Three days before Christma[s] [■■■■■■■■■■]
relaxing. Cake iced. Puddin[g] [■■■■■]
Christmas tree decorated. T[■■■■■■]
some unposted Christmas cards: important cards
which simply *must* arrive before Christmas . . .

Had it not been for that oversight, Kate and Rory
would not have had to rush down to the post-office,
taking the short cut through the lanes. They would
never have met Sam and Brigid, or been introduced to
their sick sister Ann.

And they would never have seen the glass globe in
Mrs Foley's window – the glass globe that was to lead
them into all kinds of exciting adventures over the next
two days. . . .

TONY HICKEY

The Glass Globe
ADVENTURE

Illustrated by Terry Myler

THE CHILDREN'S PRESS

First published in 1994 by
The Children's Press
45 Palmerston Road, Dublin 6

© Text: Tony Hickey 1994
© Illustrations: The Children's Press

ISBN 0 947962 87 5

Origination by Computertype Ltd.
Printed by Colour Books Ltd.

Contents

1
A Misty Night in the Lanes

It was the twenty-second of December and it seemed to Mrs Nolan, as she checked the downstairs rooms of Number Seven, Rowan Terrace, that everything was in order for the coming festivities.

The Christmas cake was iced. The pudding was made. The rest of the food was in the fridge. A fine Christmas tree, surrounded by an impressive array of colourfully wrapped parcels, stood in the sitting-room.

On the sofa, next to the tree, were the costumes for the pantomime that the local drama group was putting on on Boxing Day. Mrs Nolan had organised the making of these costumes and expected the members of the cast to collect them next morning.

On top of the desk next to the sofa were the posters advertising the disco that Mr Nolan had organised for New Year's Eve on behalf of the local junior football team. Mr Nolan managed and trained this team and the eldest Nolan son, William, aged sixteen, was its centre half.

'Yes indeed,' Mrs Nolan said, as much to herself as to her two younger children, Kate aged twelve and Rory aged ten. 'I think we can safely say that, for once, everything is nicely under control. In fact the only thing that I can see that needs to be done is to tidy the desk.'

It was then that Mrs Nolan discovered the unposted Christmas cards. 'Oh dear,' she said. 'Look at what I've just found. They got pushed in under these papers! And, of course, they would be the cards intended for your Dad's customers!'

Mr Nolan was the best carpenter in the town of Tobar

and always made a point of sending Christmas cards to the people he had worked for during the year.

'He'll be so upset when he discovers they haven't been posted. And it's as much my fault as it is his! I'm supposed to look after the paperwork!'

'No one could blame you,' said Kate in what Rory called her 'grown-up' voice. This voice usually meant she was going to try and organise things and while, as a rule, he got on fairly well with her, he did hate it when she tried to boss him around. Then her dark brown eyes would become even darker and she would smooth down her long black hair until it looked like a veil. Sometimes she would even try and smooth down *his* hair, which was as fair as hers was dark, and call him 'little brother'.

'Well she'd better not try that now,' thought Rory, getting ready to glare at her.

But, for the moment, Kate ignored him and went on talking to their mother, 'If the cards were posted this evening, they would be delivered by Christmas Eve. They're all going to people who live locally, aren't they?'

'Yes, but I have no stamps left,' said Mrs. Nolan. 'You'd never get to the post-office by six o'clock.'

'I would if I took the short cut through the lanes!'

The lanes were the poorest part of the town, narrow and winding, gloomy on even the brightest day.

'I don't like you going down there by yourself after dark!'

'Rory will come with me,' said Kate, knowing quite well that he was afraid of the dark.

'Well, in that case, all right.' Mrs Nolan took some money from the cash-box in the desk and gave it and the cards to Kate. 'Only straight there and back now.'

'Of course,' said Kate. She was out in the hall winding a scarf around her neck before Rory fully realised what she had involved him in.

'Hurry up,' was all she said to him before she rushed him out of the house.

A thick, damp river mist covered the town, turning the street decorations into mere coloured blobs. Even the star on top of the Christmas tree in the market square was barely visible. Everything looked very creepy and strange. Creepiest and strangest of all was the entrance to the lanes.

Here the mist was so thick that not a stim of light was visible, just a silent greyness. 'It's like going into a world without shape,' thought Kate.

Then the sound of Rory calling, 'Hey, wait for me!' made her realise that, instead of hurrying, she had come to a halt. If Rory caught up with her, it would spoil the reason she had suggested that he come down the lanes with her, which was not to make her mother happy but to pay Rory back for the dozen little ways he had found to annoy her and her friends since the holidays had begun.

She ran down the first of the lanes. The ground, invisible beneath her feet, had been made very slippery by the mist. She almost lost her balance and felt something very like the twinge of the fear she hoped that Rory would feel when he entered the lanes. Then she told herself to be sensible, and moved forward quickly through the mist.

Rory plunged into the lanes after her. He was quite unaware he was being punished for having irritated Kate. He saw the way that she was behaving as another attempt on her part to make him feel as though he was six years younger than her instead of just two. But, in spite of his determination not to let her get away with anything, he could not avoid feeling very, very nervous as the mist closed in around him.

The only sounds he could hear were his own footsteps. And they sounded so loud and echoey that, in spite of wanting to keep up with Kate, he stood still just to make sure that he was not surrounded by other, running figures hiding in the mist. Then he heard Kate gasp and, forgetting all his fears, he rushed forward, calling out, 'Kate, are you all right?'

Kate emerged through the mist, startlingly close to him. 'Of course I'm all right, but there's something you won't believe just around the corner.' She grabbed his arm and pulled him along beside her. 'There! What do you think of that?'

Now it was Rory's turn to gasp. A brilliant circle of golden light danced and floated on the swirling mist. Then he realised that the source of the light was the window of Mrs Foley's, one of the few shops in the lanes. A lamp had been placed there so that it shone through a glass globe which hung on silver-coloured chains from a hook in the ceiling.

The globe was the size of a small fish bowl but, instead of fish, the bowl contained a scene also made of glass. This scene showed a palm-tree and a hut, a fishing boat and a young fisherman.

'It looks like something from the West Indies,' said Rory.

'That's what I thought,' said Kate, 'but what is it doing in the window of Mrs. Foley's shop?'

'Maybe it's Mrs Foley's idea of a special Christmas display,' said Rory.

'Don't be daft! Special displays are for attracting people's attention. Not even Mrs Foley could think that anyone would be bothered looking at the rest of the stuff she has in the window.'

What Kate had said was true. Apart from the glass globe, the shop window looked exactly as it had done every other day of the year.

It was filled with old books and magazines, surrounded by soiled and dusty toys. It was a wonder to most people that Mrs Foley even bothered to keep the shop open. What few customers she ever had, had long ago deserted her for the new shopping centre.

Even before the centre had opened most people, especially young people, would have thought twice about going into Mrs Foley's shop. Her arthritis had made her very bad tempered and she was not above swinging the stick that she always carried at those whom she thought were being rude or cheeky.

'Well, if the globe is not part of a special display, maybe it's for sale,' said Rory. 'It would make a terrific wedding anniversary present for Mum and Dad in a few weeks. But there doesn't seem to be a price-tag on it, unless, of course, it fell off.'

He and Kate scanned the window for the price-tag when suddenly they remembered why they had gone down the lanes in the first place. 'The stamps for the cards!' Kate said. 'The glass globe will just have to wait until we finish at the post-office!'

Miss Green, who ran the post-office, was, as usual, full of chat. 'Last-minute rush, I see. Forgotten to post early? Ten stamps you said? All ready for this evening, are you?'

Kate and Rory stared blankly at her. 'Don't tell me you've forgotten about the carol practice in the church at half-past seven? And it organised by your own mother! I suppose you were relying on her to remind you. She's such a wonderful woman, all the things that she does!'

Kate and Rory nodded politely. They were well used to hearing their parents praised for helping with so many projects in the town but, right now, all they wanted was to get back to Mrs Foley's shop.

Neither of them spoke as they went back down the lanes. It was as though they were afraid that what they had seen would turn out to be a mirage or an illusion. But the glass globe was still there, swaying gently, touched by a draft of warm air inside the shop.

'Are we going to go in and ask if it's for sale?' queried Rory.

Before Kate could answer Rory's question, two figures emerged through the mist and came forward into the circle of golden light. Rory and Kate recognised them as Brigid and Sam Kelly who lived in the lanes. Brigid was in Kate's class at the convent. Sam was in a class lower than Rory at St Joseph's. He had a stammer which got worse when he was nervous. The four children stared shyly at each other. They had never spoken to each other outside school. Kate nodded at the glass globe and said, 'It's lovely, isn't it? How long has it been in the window?'

'O-only sin-since this aft-ternoon,' Sam said and blushed.

'We're hoping to buy it for our sister Anne,' said Brigid. 'She's been sick since October with some kind of 'flu. She has to stay in bed all the time.'

'We-we read somewhere that a-a beautiful thing can-can sometimes make a-a sick person well,' explained Sam.

Without having to discuss the matter, Kate and Rory knew that there was no way now that they could buy the glass globe for their parents.

'We were trying to get up the courage to go in and talk to Mrs Foley,' said Brigid, 'but she can be so cross! She might go for us with her stick!'

'She can hardly attack four of us at the same time,' said Kate. 'Come on!'

An old-fashioned bell rang when the shop door opened. Mrs Foley pulled back the velvet curtain that separated her living quarters from the shop. Leaning heavily on her stick, she glared at the children. 'What do you want?'

Kate said, 'We were wondering if the glass globe in the window is for sale.'

'And what if it is?'

'We were thinking maybe of buying it.'

'Oh, were you indeed! Maybe you'd like to buy the shop as well, for it's for sale along with everything in it!'

'N-no. We-we just wa-want to buy th-the globe,' said Sam.

Mrs Foley turned her beady gaze on Sam. 'Is that a real stammer or can you turn it on and off as you wish?'

'It's a real stammer,' Brigid said indignantly. 'It just gets worse when he's upset.'

'And I suppose I've upset him?'

'Well you weren't very nice to us considering that we only asked a question,' Kate said, using her grown-up voice again.

For a moment, Mrs Foley looked as though she might swing her stick at Kate. Then she laughed, amused by Kate's manner. 'Perhaps you're right. Perhaps I wasn't very civil. This damp weather makes my arthritis worse. In fact, my arthritis is the main reason why I am selling this place and going off to live with my married daughter in Dublin. Now as regards the glass globe: yes, it is for sale. I want fifty pounds for it.'

Fifty pounds! The children's faces fell.

'There's no chance you'd take less?' asked Kate.

'No chance at all. I'd get more if I wasn't anxious to get away from here as quickly as possible.'

'Why didn't you try and sell the globe sooner then?' asked Rory.

'Because I didn't even know I had it until I found it in a box when I was clearing out the attic this morning.'

'Would you give us time to try and raise the money?' asked Kate.

'Well I suppose, since the globe seems to mean so much to you, that you can have until Christmas Eve.'

'But that's the day after tomorrow,' protested Brigid.

'Take it or leave it,' said Mrs Foley.

'We'll take it,' Kate said quickly. 'And you won't sell it

to anyone else, will you?'

'Anyone else, who really wants it, won't mind waiting two days for it,' replied Mrs Foley, 'so you will be safe enough. Now off you go. I want to lock up.'

The children stepped out into the lane. Mrs Foley locked the door and switched off the light in the window, plunging the lane into darkness.

Brigid said to Kate, 'Did you mean you would help Sam and me when you asked for time to raise the fifty pounds?'

'Yes, of course,' answered Kate.

'But why would you want to help us?'

'Because it might make Anne better,' Kate said. There were many other things she felt like saying, such as it must be bad enough to live in the lanes without being sick in bed all the time. She might also have spoken of a sudden memory she had of Anne standing in the school-yard one frosty morning. Her red hair had been so warm looking, her face so pale and thin. Yet, in spite of appearing weak, she had stood up for some of the smaller girls who were being bullied by the seniors. But even if she had no memories at all of Anne, Kate knew that she and Rory were doing the right thing in helping Brigid and Sam to buy the glass globe.

'Would you like to come and see Anne?' Brigid asked.

'Do you mean right now?'

'Yes. It would cheer her up. But don't mention the glass globe. She'd only be very disappointed if we didn't manage to get it for her.'

2
Talk in Two Houses

As the children hurried along the lanes, the mist seemed to be slowly lifting. Sam and Brigid stopped outside a tall, dark house. 'This is where we live,' Brigid said.

'There are no lights on,' said Rory. 'Are your parents out? Is Anne in there all by herself?'

'No, of course she isn't!' Brigid laughed. 'When the weather is cold, Dad hangs old army blankets over the windows to keep in the heat. That's why you can't see any light.' She opened the front door and led the way down a narrow, dimly lit hall into a dark, gloomy kitchen where Mrs Kelly sat close to an old-fashioned range.

Her face brightened slightly when she saw Sam and Brigid. 'Hello. Who's that you have with you?'

'Kate and Rory Nolan,' said Brigid. 'They've come to see Anne.'

'Good. But they mustn't stay too long. She gets tired very easily.'

The stairs that led up to Anne's room were as steep as a step-ladder. The window on the landing, shrouded in a blanket, increased the feeling of poverty and gloom. Kate and Rory had never imagined a house could be so depressing. Then they entered Anne's room and it was like being transported to a different world. An electric fire filled with the room with warmth. A bedside lamp with a pink shade cast its light on a bright patchwork quilt. Propped up in a bed against snow-white pillows was Anne, her red hair shining like silk.

Brigid said, 'Rory and Kate have come to visit.'

Anne smiled. 'Good,' she said. 'Kate, you're in Brigid's

class, aren't you? And Rory is in a class ahead of Sam.'

'You've a very good memory,' said Rory.

'I play a game that helps me to remember. I imagine all the classrooms and who is in which class and what lessons they might be doing.'

'Did Dr Redmond call while we were out?' asked Brigid.

'Yes, he did. He thinks that I might have to go into hospital in the new year. Do you know Dr Redmond?' Anne asked the Nolans.

'Yes, we do,' said Kate. 'In fact his daughter, Honor, is kind of our brother William's girl-friend.'

'Is Honor nice?'

'Oh yes, although I don't know why she's suddenly so interested in William. They've known each other for ever but never paid any attention to each other until she came on holiday from boarding-school a few days ago,' said Kate.

'Maybe that's what's meant by falling in love,' Anne said in such a wistful voice that they all realised how lonely she must be, almost like a fairy princess in a room at the top of a tower.

'I think it's gross the way they keep looking at each other and holding hands,' said Rory, who, apart from feeling sorry for Anne, did not want the conversation to get too soppy.

Fortunately Sam came to his rescue. He said, 'I think I heard Dad coming in.'

There was a murmur of voices downstairs as Mr Kelly greeted his wife. Then he hurried upstairs to Anne's room. His eyes looked sad and tired but he made an effort to sound cheerful when he saw the visitors. 'So we've got a full house this evening! Dave Nolan is your father, isn't he? I've seen you all at Mass together. Lucky man, your father! Never out of work! I wish I'd had the sense to become a carpenter!'

'You had no luck looking for work around the town then?' asked Anne.

'No, but, even if there was a job going, it would be given to someone else. It seems we are still outsiders even though we've lived here for ten years!' Then, as if realising that he might be upsetting Anne, he managed to smile again and said, 'But who knows? Something might turn up.'

Anne tried to smile back but suddenly she looked even more pale.

'We'd best go,' said Kate. 'We'll be late for our tea and there's a carol practice in the church at half-past seven.' Then she had an idea. 'Why don't you and Sam come to it? It's for a good cause. We'll be going out tomorrow to collect money for famine victims.'

Brigid and Sam looked at their father. 'Go, if you want to,' he said.

When they were back once more in the lanes, Rory said to Kate, 'I'm glad you asked Sam and Brigid to the carol practice. It might make them feel as though they belong in Tobar.'

'Yes. But, remember, not a word to anyone about the glass globe to anyone.'

'What do you take me for, a baby?'

Kate suddenly felt mischievous. 'Yes,' she said. 'A baby that's afraid of the dark. What's that behind you?'

As Rory spun around in alarm, Kate took off and ran out into the side street where she almost collided with her best friend, Madge Cronin. 'Where are you coming from?' Madge demanded.

'The Kellys,' gasped Kate. 'We went to see Anne.'

Madge was surprised. 'You do know that they can't find out what's wrong with her? And her father never does any work.'

'He was out looking for work today.'

'My father says there are plenty of jobs available.'

'Then maybe he could find one for Mr. Kelly,' said Rory, who had arrived in time to hear what had been said.

'I'm not talking to you,' Madge snapped. She and Rory disliked each other.

'All the same, Rory is right,' said Kate. 'Mr Kelly *is* looking for work. Maybe we shouldn't be so hard on him and on the other people who live in the lanes.'

Madge was amazed. She and Kate were having their first disagreement in ages and all over the Kellys! Not only that but Kate was siding with Rory! Maybe Kate needed time to come to her senses. She said very snootily, 'I'll see you at the carol practice,' and walked away before Kate could say anything else that would turn the disagreement into a serious quarrel.

Rory was full of admiration for Kate. 'You were great,' he said, but, in spite of praising her, he had not forgotten the fright that she had given him in the lanes. 'Last home is a wombat!' Off he rushed, leaving Kate standing, but she soon caught up with him.

They arrived back in Rowan Terrace at the same time as William and their father. Mrs Nolan looked out from the kitchen. 'All home together for a change! That makes things a lot easier. Tea in ten minutes. Everyone washes their hands, including you,' she said to her husband.

'Don't you want to hear my news first?' Mr Nolan asked.

'No, first I want all of you here in the kitchen ready to eat. We don't want to be late for the carol practice.'

William groaned, 'Is that this evening?'

'Yes, it is. And you had better be there!'

'Along with Honor Redmond, of course,' Mr Nolan said teasingly, getting to the bathroom before William.

Rory and Kate washed their hands in the kitchen.

'Did you post the cards all right?' Mrs Nolan asked.

'Yes,' said Kate. 'I'll give you your change in a second.'

"Just put it back in the box. Oh, and there's no need to say anything to your Dad about the cards almost being forgotten.'

Kate and Rory grinned at each other. It seemed to be a day for secrets. And there was still Dad's news to hear.

'We asked Sam and Brigid Kelly to the carol practice,' Kate said.

'Just as long as they can sing,' Mrs Nolan said vaguely. Her attention was on the food cooking in the oven.

'That smells delicious,'said Mr Nolan, coming back into the kitchen and giving her a big hug. 'What is it?'

'Your favourite: fishcakes.'

'With mashed potatoes and peas?'

'Absolutely,' said Mrs Nolan. 'Where's William?'

'Combing his hair to please Honor,' said Mr Nolan.

'Just as long as he washed his hands too.'

'Would you like to inspect them?' William held out his hands as he came in from the hall and took his place at the table.

As soon as the food had been served and approved of with great smacking of lips, Mrs Nolan said to her husband, 'So what's all this news you have for us?'

'Miss Freeman is back.'

Mrs Nolan was truly surprised at the announcement. 'Back in the old Freeman house do you mean, or just visiting Tobar?'

'Back in the old Freeman house and probably back for some time. She called in to see me about doing some repair work. I drove out to the house with her this afternoon.'

'You were actually in the Freeman house?' William, who tried to be cool about most things, was very impressed. The Freeman house had long been a talking point in Tobar. It was situated three miles outside the town, surrounded by a high wall and tall beech-trees. There were all kinds of stories told of the strange and terrible things that were supposed to have happened there since it had been built two hundred years ago. Even the most daring of the young people steered clear of the place. Just to look through its metal gates and down the long, weed-clogged avenue was enough to send a chill down most backs. When adults talked about it, it was usually in hushed voices. All that Rory and Kate knew for certain about it was that it was a house of mystery and strange rumours.

'What was it like inside?' asked William.

'Dark and gloomy and sadly in need of repair,' said Mr Nolan, 'although in a way I should be happy about that. It means there's more than enough work to keep me going there until Easter. You could pitch in and give me a hand if you like. It would be valuable work experience.'

William was studying to be a carpenter at the vocational

school. 'Would I get paid for the work?'

Mr Nolan sighed. 'Yes, you'll get paid for it.'

William said, 'It's not just greed. A group of us are thinking of starting a band. We'll have to buy equipment.'

'I don't like the sound of that,' said Mrs Nolan.

'You haven't even heard us play yet,' protested William.

'I wasn't thinking of your band. I was thinking of Miss Freeman all by herself in that house.

'She's not using the whole house, just three of the downstairs bedrooms. She's made a kind of flat with a kitchen and, I suppose, what must have been the breakfast-room and a room off it, she's turned into a bedroom,' said Mr Nolan.

'Those were the housekeeper's rooms,' said Mrs Freeman.

'How do you know that?' asked William.

'I used to go out there as a child to play with Miss Freeman.'

'You never told us about that before,' said Kate.

'There never seemed to be any need to, especially with the house closed up and Miss Freeman living abroad. It all seems so far away now anyway.'

'Miss Freeman asked especially about you,' said Mr Nolan. 'She wants us all to go to tea tomorrow. I said you'd let her know. Someone will have to go out there with a note. Her telephone isn't connected yet.'

Mrs Nolan was not too happy at the idea. 'Maybe it would be better if she came in here.'

'Are you not sure you're not afraid to go out there?' asked William.

'Do you mean because of all the stories and tales told about the place?' Mrs Nolan smiled.

'Don't tell me none of them is true!'

Mrs Nolan laughed. 'Would you be very disappointed to know that we don't have the equivalent of Dracula's

Castle on the outskirts of the town? Oh, I daresay some sad and terrible things did happen there since the house was built but they were long over by my time. I was invited out there to play with Adelaide – Miss Freeman – because the housekeeper knew your Granny, God rest the two of them! Going there was always so strict! Mr and Mrs Freeman were elderly and Miss Freeman was their only child. I used to feel so sorry for her! All that money and no one to share it with!'

'Where did the Freeman money come from?' William asked.

'I don't know. They always just seemed to have plenty of it. When Adelaide was old enough, she was sent to school in Switzerland and almost never came back to Tobar. I was growing up myself by then and I would just occasionally catch sight of her being driven around by the chauffeur in her father's car. Both her parents died abroad. I wrote to her when I heard and got a very nice letter in reply. We haven't been in touch since.'

'Well, she seems very anxious to resume the friendship,' Mr Nolan said as he finished off the last of his fishcakes. 'I think she really would appreciate it if we all went out there tomorrow.'

'Well, in that case, I suppose we'd better go,' Mrs Nolan said. 'The only reason I resisted was that I didn't want her to go to too much trouble.'

3
Plans are Made

Madge Cronin was already in the choir loft when the Nolans got there as were most of the other singers, including Miss Green from the post-office and Mrs Hughes and her daughter Sylvia, who was the princess in the pantomime.

Both Sylvia and her mother had great hopes of Sylvia becoming a movie star. In fact, they both behaved as though she already was one.

Madge gave Kate a 'no-hard-feelings' kind of nod and held out the book of words for her to share.

Then Sam and Brigid Kelly came into the choir loft.

'Who invited them?' demanded Madge.

'I did,' said Kate, beckoning to Brigid to join them while Sam went over to where Rory was with his two best friends, Joe Deegan and Arthur Molloy.

Mr Morris, the church organist, raised his hand and the singing began. The first carol was 'Silent Night'. Madge held the book of words as far as she could from Brigid but Brigid didn't need the book. Neither did Sam. They knew the words and were so carried away that they did not notice when Mr Morris signalled to everyone else to be quiet so that the two Kellys finished the carol by themselves.

'That was excellent,' said Mr Morris. 'Where did you learn to sing like that?'

Sam, shy at having everyone look at him, let Brigid answer the question. 'At home,' she said. 'We always sing carols at Christmas.'

'Well, if your parents are half as good as the two of you,

please ask them to join the choir. We could do with some new voices.'

Madge could not believe her ears. Mrs Hughes and Sylvia did not look too pleased either at the two children from the lanes being praised in this way.

But Kate and Rory were delighted. So were Sam and Brigid. They had never before felt so much part of the town of Tobar.

'Carol number two, "Away in a Manger",' said Mr Morris.

Once more, Sam and Brigid sang so sweetly that Mrs Nolan thought to herself, 'It's like hearing the words for the first time.' She and her husband smiled at each other. They smiled even more when they saw how closely Honor and William were standing together, their heads almost touching over their book of words.

When the last carol was sung, Mr Morris declared himself satisfied and reminded the singers that they were to meet on the next evening at six-thirty outside the church. He said, 'Mr Rice from the garage has, as usual, kindly offered to drive us around in his open lorry. But, please, wrap up warmly. Now, safe home to all of you!'

Madge, still sulking, left the choir loft without a word to Kate and Brigid. Mrs Hughes and Sylvia cornered Mrs Nolan and insisted that they be allowed to call around later to try on Sylvia's costume for the pantomime.

Mr O'Connor, the director of the pantomime, was waiting for Mr Nolan with the plans for the scenery. He said, 'I'm sorry to land you with this, but Basil Byrne, who was going to build the scenery, has the 'flu.'

'How much is there to be done?' asked Mr Nolan.

'Well, all of it,' said Mr O'Connor. 'Basil got sick before he started.'

'I see,' said Mr Nolan. 'Well in that case, you'd better come back to the house and explain it all to me.' He called out to William, 'I need you to help me with this.'

'Honor and I said we'd meet the others for coffee,' protested William.

'You can drink coffee at home,' said Mrs Nolan. 'Maybe Honor will help me to sort out the costumes.'

'Well if you really need help . . .' said Honor.

'That's settled then,' said Mrs Nolan.

Kate drew Brigid to one side. 'I think you and Sam should come back to our house too. With William and Dad busy with the scenery, and Mum and Honor in the front room with the costumes, it's the perfect time to make plans for buying the glass globe. Go and get Sam and Rory away from Joe and Arthur.'

Brigid turned back to where the four boys were fooling around, pretending to push each other off the pavement. Kate slipped in beside her mother and asked, 'Can Sam and Brigid come back for a while?'

'I don't see why not. It looks as though half the town will be there eventually. Here's the front door key. You may have some biscuits and orange juice but no crumbs in your bedroom!'

'We'll be careful,' promised Kate. 'Come on,' she said to Brigid and Sam and Rory.

'What about us?' asked Joe and Arthur.

'Not tonight,' Kate said.

'Thanks a lot,' said Joe. He and Rory and Arthur had recently formed The Three Demolishers' Pact, based on their favourite characters in their favourite comic. They didn't think much of being ditched by Rory but there was no way that he could explain without giving away the secret of the glass globe. 'They'll understand when I'm allowed to tell them,' he thought, as he hurried after Kate.

As soon as the four of them were settled down in her bedroom, Kate reached for a notebook and pencil. 'We have to know how much money we can provide ourselves and how much we need to raise.'

'Sam and I have four pounds fifty between us. That's all we were able to save. We were hoping to buy a present for our parents but the globe is more important.'

'I can give five pounds,' said Rory.

'And I can manage the same,' said Kate, writing the figures down and adding them up. 'That comes to fourteen pounds fifty, which means that we need to raise thirty-five pounds fifty. Does anyone have any ideas?'

There was silence for several minutes, apart, that is, from the sound of biscuits being chewed and juice being drunk. Then Kate sucked the end of her pencil. 'We need to get into the service industries,' she said.

'How do you mean?' asked Rory.

'I mean we should look for jobs that are not too hard to do but that people don't like to do for themselves. Window-cleaning would be a good example.'

'Window-cleaning isn't that easy,' said Rory. 'Remember what happened to Frank Mooney when he was cleaning the windows at the convent. He fell off his ladder and broke his leg.'

'We'll only do one-storey houses,' said Kate. 'There are those new bungalows out near the old quarry. Mainly elderly people live there. I bet they'd be delighted to have their windows cleaned in time for Christmas.'

'How much should we charge?' asked Rory.

Kate examined the figures she had written down. 'How many windows are there to each bungalow?' she asked.

Rory tried to remember what the bungalows looked like. Finally he had a guess. 'Eight or nine.'

'Eight or nine!' Kate was delighted. 'We only need to do four bungalows and charge less than one pound per window. Of course we would have to spend something on equipment. We'll need cloths and buckets and a long-handled mop and window-cleaning liquid. I suggest that

we meet tomorrow morning at nine o'clock, with our money, behind the courthouse in the market square. We can then split up and buy what we need without attracting too much attention.'

'I read in the paper the other day about a fellow in England who started off cleaning windows,' said Rory. 'He's now a millionaire.'

'Maybe we'll end up as millionaires too,' said Kate. 'But one thing is certain. By this time tomorrow, the glass globe will be ours!'

Shivers of excitement ran through the four of them. Brigid said, 'We'll put the globe in a box, wrap it up and give it to Anne on Christmas Day!'

Kate filled their mugs with the last of the orange juice and said, 'To the Window-Cleaners of Tobar!'

'To the Window-Cleaners of Tobar,' the other three replied.

They drained their mugs and were about to go on talking when Mrs Nolan knocked on the door. 'It's getting late,' she said. 'I don't want Mr and Mrs Kelly to start worrying about Sam and Brigid.'

'They're just leaving,' Kate called back.

Mrs Nolan waited in the hall as the Kellys put on their coats. She couldn't help noticing how worn they were and how Sam had almost grown out of his. 'Go straight home now,' she said.

'We will,' said Brigid. 'Thanks for the biscuits and the orange juice.'

'Good-bye.'

'Good-bye.'

The words of farewell hung briefly on the air as the Kellys hurried away from the house. Then Mrs Hughes and Sylvia arrived. 'I hope we are not too late to try on Sylvia's costume,' Mrs Hughes said.

Kate and Rory had an attack of the giggles at the thought of Mrs Hughes and Sylvia trying to get into the same costume, and fled back upstairs where they rolled around with laughter in Kate's room until Mrs Nolan came up to them and said angrily, 'Behave yourselves! We can hear you downstairs!'

Long after all the visitors had gone and the house was in darkness, Kate and Rory remained wide-awake and wished it was morning. When at last Rory did go to sleep, he dreamed of buckets and mops and cloths, all cleaning windows by themselves.

4
Getting Away Safely

At breakfast next morning the conversation was, at first, all about the pantomime. Mr Nolan insisted that not only William but also Kate and Rory should help with the making of the scenery, which was due to begin in the main hall of the community centre that evening.

'And Honor can give me a hand with Sylvia Hughes's costume,' said Mrs Nolan. 'The waist measurements were written down as the arm measurements. The result is the sleeves are far too short and the waist is far too big.'

'In that case it might fit her mother,' said William. 'Mrs Hughes would be a sensation as the princess!'

'Just as you would be if you ever said something sensible,' said Mrs Nolan, and then, in spite of her intention to be serious, began to laugh at the idea of Mrs Hughes as the princess.

'What about this tea-party at Miss Freeman's?' asked her husband.

'I'll go into the sitting-room now and write her a note to say that we will be there,' replied Mrs Nolan.

'And I want to go over the plans for the pantomime scenery again,' said Mr Nolan. 'William, you'd better come and have a look at them as well.'

As soon as William and their parents had left the kitchen, Kate said, 'Let's get out of here before they find something for us to do this morning.'

Brigid and Sam were waiting for them behind the courthouse. They all grinned with excitement, 'It's desperate co-cold,' said Sam.

'That's good,' said Kate. 'We should find plenty of

people at home. Elderly people don't go out much in cold weather. Did you bring your money?'

Brigid handed over their money.

'Good,' said Kate. 'Now I think we should split up to do the shopping. That way we won't attract too much attention. I'll buy one bucket at Morgan's. Brigid can buy the second one at Fogarty's.'

'I looked in Morgan's on my way here. The buckets cost three pounds each,' said Brigid.

'While you two buy the buckets I could buy the long-handled mop at the DIY place,' said Rory. 'Sam could buy the cloths and the cleaning liquid in one of the super-markets. We could be ready to leave in a few minutes.'

Kate divided the money between them. Then she and Brigid left the market square.

The boys waited a while before going off on their errands.

Rory was almost at the DIY shop when the sound of Honor Redmond's voice startled him, 'Are you looking for Kate? I saw her going into Morgan's.' The expression on Rory's face surprised her. 'Is there something wrong?'

Before Rory could think what to say Kate came out of Morgan's carrying a blue plastic bucket. Almost immediately Brigid, carrying a yellow plastic bucket, came running down the street, followed by Madge Cronin.

Close on Madge's heels came Sam, who managed to gasp as he ran by, 'She's after us!'

Madge Cronin skidded to a halt beside Kate and glared at the blue bucket. 'Why are you and Brigid Kelly buying buckets?' she demanded. 'Brigid Kelly was sneaking around in Fogarty's as though she was going to steal something! Then that twerp of a brother of hers came along, saw me and rushed in and warned her that she was being watched. She just dumped some money on the counter, grabbed a bucket and rushed off without even getting a

receipt! What do you make of that?'

'As long as she paid for it, what's the difference?' Kate said, determined to remain calm.

'There's a lot of difference between shopping properly and sneaking around shops,' replied Madge. 'I want to know what's going on!'

Rory felt a sudden surge of courage. 'I forbid Kate to answer that question!'

Madge's eyes bulged. 'No one is talking to you, you little brat!'

'Maybe not, but I still forbid Kate to answer your question!'

Madge looked at Kate, expecting her to contradict Rory. Instead Kate said, in a very soft voice, 'I'm sorry, Madge. What Rory has said is true. I cannot talk without his permission.'

Madge's eyes bulged even further. She began to splutter

and squeak. 'You'll be sorry for this, Kate Nolan!' She headed off down the street.

Honor said, 'What on earth is going on?'

'We can't tell you,' Kate said. 'But please, please, don't say anything to William about what happened just now.'

'All right,' promised Honor. 'Where is William?'

'At home,' said Rory. 'If you hurry, you'll catch him.'

As soon as Honor was out of earshot, Kate said to Rory, 'Go and buy the mop before Madge comes back. And remember, try not to attract too much attention!'

Not attracting attention was very hard since the long-handled mop was taller than he was and difficult to carry. Before he'd even got out of the shop, he had banged into several people and almost knocked over a pyramid of paint tins.

On the street it was even more difficult, like trying to carry a fishing-line without catching anyone on the hook. To add to his problems, he met Arthur and Joe, who wanted him to practise goal-kicking on the football pitch.

'I can't,' he said. 'I'm busy.'

'You won't be busy after you leave that mop at home,' said Joe.

'It's a bit more complicated than that,' Rory said.

'Oh, I see,' said Arthur. 'Like last night when we didn't get asked back to your house after the carol practice. What about The Demolishers' Pact? The sign of one that one is for two and two is for three? United against the world?'

Rory switched the mop on his other shoulder and narrowly avoided removing the postman's hat. 'I know we said we wouldn't have any secrets,' he said. 'But I just can't tell you what's going on now. But I will be able to this evening. In fact,' he said, thinking of the plans for becoming millionaires, 'there could eventually be a lot of money in it for us all!'

The mention of money did the trick. Joe and Arthur

agreed to wait for the answers to their question until after the carol singing. Then, to show that there was no hard feeling, the three boys repeated the words of The Demolisher and his friends and exchanged the special handshake. 'Sign of one, sign of two, sign of three!'

'So now it's a mop, is it?' Madge, flushed with anger, was back. Obviously she had failed to catch up with the Kellys. Kate must also have escaped.

'Enemy within reach!' Rory cried in his Demolisher's voice. 'Stop and detain!'

Arthur and Joe joined hands, trapping Madge between them. 'Let me go!' she shrieked. 'Let me go!'

Rory grasped the mop as though it were a lance and charged down the main street and back towards the market square. Sam, carrying a supermarket bag, appeared as if from nowhere and joined in the gallop. Together they pranced around the back of the courthouse.

'The danger is past,' Rory, still being The Demolisher, said to the two girls. 'Madge has been taken prisoner by my trusted allies.'

'What does he mean "Madge has been taken prisoner?"', asked Brigid.

'Playing games as usual,' replied Kate. 'But, at least, no one is following us.'

They climbed the wall that separated the market square from the countryside and set off across the fields to Quarry Road and the bungalows.

5

A Terrible Mistake

Kate rang the bell of the first bungalow and waited. Nothing happened. She rang again after a few minutes. Still nothing happened. 'They must be out,' she said. 'Let's try next door.'

Rory rang the bell on the second house. There was a heart-stopping outburst of barking from inside the hall, followed by a thud as some huge dog flung itself against the front door.

'I don't think we should disturb these people,' Rory said.

They went to the third bungalow. Here Sam rang the bell. A muffled shout came from inside the house.

'I think someone is telling us to hold on,' Sam said.

He was right. Within seconds, chains were drawn back, locks released and the front door opened by a sleepy-eyed bald man in a dressing-gown. He looked at the children. 'You are not the postman,' he said accusingly.

'No,' said Kate. 'We're the window-cleaners.'

'You're the what?'

'The window-cleaners!'

'The WHAT?'

Rory was suddenly inspired. 'WINDOWS' he shouted. 'CLEANING. Like this!' He pretended to squeeze the long-handled mop and to dab at the glass panels on the front door. The man backed away in alarm. 'Clear off!' he ordered. 'Clear off or I'll call the guards! Vandals! Hooligans!'

'NO, NO,' protested Kate. 'YOU'VE GOT IT ALL WRONG!'

But the bald man had slammed and relocked the door before Kate finished speaking.

'We're not doing very well,' Rory said gloomily.

'But at least other people know why we're here,' Brigid said. 'While you and that man were shouting at each other, curtains were flicked back in some of the other bungalows!'

'Then we might as well try next door,' said Kate. 'It's your turn to ring the bell.'

Brigid gave the bell three short rings. She thought that sounded more friendly than one longish ring. She seemed to have guessed right, for the door was opened at once by a smiling grey-haired woman who said, 'Well now, a happy Christmas to you all. And aren't you right good to come out on a day like this! I heard what happened next door. Don't worry! He's a bit deaf and that makes him cross. But now, tell me what do you need before you start work?'

'Some hot water,' Kate said.

'Well if you don't mind, I'll ask you to come around to the back door for that,' the woman said. 'Your shoes are a bit muddy. You must have come across the fields. I am Mrs Brown. Who are you?'

The children introduced themselves and felt so delighted at how well their plans were suddenly working that they almost did a little dance as they held the buckets under the tap.

The buckets, when filled with warm water, were quite heavy. The boys carried one out to the front garden while the girls coped with the second one.

'How-how do we begin?' asked Sam.

Rory and Kate had often seen William and their father clean the windows at home so they knew exactly how to start. First they wiped them with a damp cloth. Then they squeezed some cleaning liquid on another cloth, attached it to the mop and smeared it over the windows.

They allowed the liquid to dry for two minutes. Then they dipped the mop in the warm water and wiped off the liquid.

To clean the outside windows of Mrs Brown's bungalow took fifteen minutes. 'Our shoes are muddier than ever now,' said Rory. 'How are we going to do the inside of the windows?'

'We will take our shoes and boots off,' Kate said, ringing the bell.

Mrs Brown opened the front door. 'I've just telephoned Mrs Grey in number eight across the road.'

The children looked across the road. Mrs Grey, all dressed in blue, waved at them from her front room.

'She was wondering if you could do her windows next. She has to go out in a few minutes. Her son will be calling for her in his car.'

'Yes, all right,' said Kate. 'Then can we do the inside of your windows if we take our shoes off?'

'Of course you can, pet,' said Mrs Brown. 'And I will have a nice pot of tea and some freshly baked currant buns all ready for you by the time you get back!'

'Thank you very much,' beamed Kate, leading the group across to number eight.

'We haven't agreed on a price yet,' Rory said.

For a second, Kate was worried. Then she said, 'Oh, there's bound to be a fixed price.'

'Supposing it's a low fixed price,' said Rory.

'It couldn't be less than one pound per window.'

'All the same, Rory is right,' said Brigid. 'Maybe we should fix a price before we do Mrs Grey's windows.'

But there was no chance to have a discussion with Mrs Grey, who was trying to finish wrapping her Christmas presents. 'Such a rush,' she kept saying. 'Such a rush! It's the same every year. And my son hates to be kept waiting.

Oh dear, such a rush! Please come in and take whatever you need.'

'Just some clean water,' Kate said as the two boys emptied the now dirty water out of the buckets. 'Could you open the back door? That way we won't dirty your carpets with our shoes.'

'Such thoughtful children! It's such a relief to get the windows cleaned for Christmas! Brightens the whole house up!' Mrs Grey clicked off to open the back door.

As soon as she had done this, she clicked back down the hall, saying, 'Now let me know when you've finished. I just must finish wrapping this ray-gun for my grandson. Oh dear, such a rush! Such a rush!'

Clearly this was not the moment to distract Mrs Grey with talk of money. They would have to concentrate on getting the job finished before her son came to collect her.

The four of them were, by now, working as a team. One wiped. One squeezed. One dried. One shone. They were finished Mrs Grey's outside windows in twelve minutes according to Kate's watch.

'We might get it down to ten minutes yet,' said Kate. 'I'll just call and see if it's all right for us to do the insides. Mrs Grey? Mrs Grey?'

Mrs Grey came fussing out of the living-room. 'Yes, dear, what is it? Don't tell me my son is here already.'

Before Kate could reply, the telephone rang, making Mrs Grey scream slightly. She picked up the receiver. 'Hello . . . Oh Mrs White . . . Yes, yes, they are . . . I will, of course . . .' She hung up and said, 'That was Mrs White in number ten. She wanted to make sure that you would do her windows next.'

'Sam and Rory could start on the outside while we finish in here,' Kate said and gave the boys one of the buckets.

Before Kate could bring up the question of money, Mrs

Grey had trotted off into her bedroom muttering some-thing about having to decide on which overcoat she should wear. Brigid turned to Kate. 'We ought to follow her in there and get this question of price settled.'

'Wait till she has her coat on. She'll be less fussed then,' replied Kate as she carried the bucket of water into the living-room. 'We'll need something to put this down on. There was a pile of newspapers by the back door.'

Brigid ran to fetch some of them. As she went back past the bedroom, Mrs Grey came out. 'Do you think this hat goes with this coat?'

'They go just great together,' Brigid said. 'We were wondering if we couldn't agree now . . .' She had intended to finish with 'on a price for cleaning the windows' but Mrs Grey went back into her bedroom and Kate called out from the front room, 'Brigid, what's keeping you? My arms are broken trying to hold this bucket.'

'Sorry,' Brigid rushed into the front room. 'I was talking to Mrs Grey.' She spread the newspapers in a thick layer on the carpet.

Kate placed the bucket on them. 'Did you agree on a price?'

'I didn't get a chance. She is just so fussed. In fact, I don't think I ever saw such a fussed woman. And putting her coat on seems to have made her worse, not better.'

'We will just have to wait until we are finished,' said Kate.

The girls set to work, moving from the living-room to the bathroom to the dining-room, to the two bedrooms and, finally, to the kitchen. They kept meeting Mrs Grey but she always flitted past them like some kind of confused twittering bird, saying things like, 'Such good children! Such kind children! Oh dear now, where did I put . . .'

Finished at last, the girls emptied the bucket and

prepared to pin Mrs Grey down and clear up the question of payment. But, even as they found her in the front room trying to put her presents into too small a bag, there was the blare of a car horn outside the house. Mrs Grey gave another startled scream. 'Oh, that must be my son, John! Be an angel and let him in!'

Kate hurried to the front door and opened it. A tall, sour-faced man was getting out of a large car. 'Who are you?' he asked quite rudely.

'I'm Kate Nolan,' Kate said. Brigid looked over her shoulder. 'And this is Brigid Kelly.'

'What are you doing in my mother's bungalow?'

'Cleaning the windows.'

Mrs Grey came fussily down the hall. 'Oh John, I'm really and truly ready to go so there will be no delay! I see you've met these two young ladies who've been cleaning my windows.'

'I hope they've done a better job than those lads across the road.' John Grey pointed at Rory and Sam, who were experiencing unexpected problems. The long-handled mop had become entangled in the branches of a cherry-tree. The more they tried to release it, the more caught up it became. To make matters worse, Rory tripped over the bucket of water and fell into a bed of rose-bushes.

'Oh dear,' said Mrs Grey. 'Mrs White thinks the world of her roses!'

A loud cry confirmed what Mrs Grey had said. The front door of number ten was flung open and Mrs White rushed out. 'Oh you clumsy boy! Get out of my roses!'

Rory did his best to obey her but the spilled water had made the path very slippery and he toppled over again, this time bringing Sam down with him.

Mrs Brown, who had been keeping on eye out for the children's return, hurried out of her bungalow. 'Oh dear, are you all right?'

'Of course they are all right,' said Mrs White, yanking both boys to their feet with a surprising show of strength in a woman of her age. 'But what about my roses? Not to mention my cherry-tree! Who is going to get that mop-head down out of it?'

The two boys stared in horror at the cherry-tree. The mop-head was still tangled in its branches. But the long handle had snapped. 'It must have broken when I slipped,' said Rory.

'Well, it can't stay up there,' said Mrs White. 'I'm surprised at the Junior Chamber of Commerce sending such young people out to do this work!'

'So am I,' said John Grey, 'Just look at the mess they've made of the windows!'

They all looked at the outside of the windows that had been cleaned. Where only a few minutes ago the glass had shone and sparkled, now all the panes were streaked and cloudy. 'The air is so cold that the water and the cleaning fluid are starting to freeze,' said John Grey. 'The Junior Chamber of Commerce should have had more sense.' Then, seeing the looks on the children's faces, he said, 'You *are* from the Junior Chamber of Commerce, aren't you?'

'No,' said Rory.

John Grey became even less friendly-looking. 'You're here under false pretences then!'

'No, we're not!' said Kate. 'We don't even know what you mean when you ask us if we're from the Junior Chamber of Commerce.'

'Then I'll explain,' John Grey said grimly. 'The Junior Chamber of Commerce, which is made up of the young business people of the town of Tobar, decided at its last meeting that it would ask for volunteers to do odd jobs to help the elderly people of the district during the Christmas period. The cleaning of windows was one of the jobs suggested. When you lot turned up here today, naturally the residents of the bungalows thought you were part of the volunteers organised by the Junior Chamber of Commerce. But now it seems that you are not. Perhaps you would care to tell us exactly who you are!'

'We just thought it would be a good way to earn some money,' Rory said.

'By exploiting old people?' John Grey said angrily.

This time Mrs Brown spoke up for the children. 'Oh now, I'm sure they never meant to do that! It was all a misunderstanding, as much on our part as on theirs . . . none of us bothered to ask who had sent them. Clean, dry newspapers will put the windows right in just a jiffy. And I'm sure that Mrs White has a step-ladder handy so that the boys can get the mop-head down out of the tree.'

'Then let them do so. Mother, we'll be late. You'd better lock up the house,' said John Grey.

'Our shoes are in the kitchen,' Brigid said.

'And our bucket is in the front room,' said Kate.

'Then I suggest you get them without delay,' said John Grey.

The girls ran down the hall and grabbed the bucket from the living-room, emptied it into the kitchen sink and struggled back into their shoes while Mrs Grey locked and bolted the back door. 'Such a mix-up,' she said. 'Such a terrible mix-up! Thank heavens my son John came along when he did!'

'I think your son John is a horrid person, a real bully,' declared Kate and then realised that John Grey was standing behind her.

'Consider yourself lucky that you aren't in even more serious trouble,' he said.

Kate tossed her head defiantly and looked at Mrs Grey. 'Is it all right if we take those old newspapers with us to wipe the windows?'

'Of course, dear,' said Mrs Grey. 'Take anything you like.'

John Grey bundled his mother and her parcels into his car and drove off.

Mrs White shook her head disapprovingly. 'He is always so cross.' Then she looked at Rory and Sam and sighed. 'Come on. I'll show you where the step-ladder is. It's not very heavy.'

Mrs White was right. The step-ladder was light to carry and easy to hold steady against the tree. Rory brought the top of the mop down.

'You can easily stick that handle back on with tape,' Mrs White said.

'And now for that cup of tea I promised you,' said Mrs Brown. 'You'll come and have one as well, won't you, Mrs White?'

'Of course I will,' replied Mrs White.

Crowded into Mrs Brown's kitchen, eating her delicious scones and drinking sweet hot tea, made the children feel somewhat better. 'We'll wipe the windows with the newspaper we got in Mrs Grey's,' said Brigid. 'We're sorry if we upset you, Mrs White.'

'I just got a fright when I saw the two lads fall into the rose-bushes,' said Mrs White. 'And I was afraid that they might break that branch off the cherry-tree.' She looked at the two boys. 'You didn't hurt yourselves, I hope?'

'Just a few scratches,' Rory said. 'And a bit of mud.'

'Don't brush it until it dries,' advised Mrs Brown. 'That's always the best thing to do with mud.'

'Yes, Mrs Brown,' Rory said.

When the last of the scones were eaten and the teapot was quite empty, Mrs White said, 'It seems only fair that we give you a reward for all your hard work.'

'We can't take money from you,' Kate said. 'It wouldn't be right.' The others nodded in agreement.

Mrs Brown and Mrs White were about to protest. Then they realised that the children were serious and not only serious but certain that they were doing the right thing.

'Well, if you feel that strongly about it, we won't force you,' said Mrs Brown. 'But there's no need for you to wipe the windows with newspaper. Let the real window-cleaners do that when they get here!'

'And let's hope we recognise them this time.' Mrs White stood up, ready to go back to her own bungalow. 'Did you want to earn money for a very special reason? Something to do with Christmas?'

'Yes,' said Kate, 'but we'll manage.'

Sadly the four children left Quarry Road. Kate thought bitterly of their talk of becoming teenage millionaires. Now it looked as though they would not be even able to buy the glass globe.

Rory said, 'We may as well walk back to Tobar by the road, seeing as how we are no longer in any kind of a hurry.'

6
Galloping Turkeys

With every step they took, the buckets and cloths and the pieces of the mop seemed to get heavier and heavier. They had left the bottle of cleaning liquid behind at the bungalows but there seemed no point in going back for that now.

'There must be something we can do,' Kate said, unable to face total defeat.

At that moment, a woman carrying a stick came running around the bend in the road. Her hair stood out around her head like a strange hat. Her feet moved uneasily in wellington boots. She wore an apron over a jumper and skirt. Her face was red. Her breath came in big, foggy gasps. She shouted at the children, 'Have you seen them? Have you seen them?'

'Seen what?' asked Rory.

'The turkeys! The turkeys!' The woman's eyes rolled in horror and dismay. 'I was walking them along the road and now they've vanished.'

Kate's mind suddenly began to tick. 'Why were you taking them for a walk?'

'I was taking them to the priest's house,' the woman said. 'His housekeeper, Mrs Melia, never serves a mouthful of turkey that doesn't come from my farmyard. And being Christmas, she ordered two. I promised her that I would get them to her by twelve o'clock. Now what am I to do?'

'T-turkeys can't j-just vanish,' said Sam.

'I didn't mean vanish like POOF! and they were suddenly gone,' said the woman.

44

'What did you mean then?' asked Brigid.

'I meant that I was on the way to the town with the turkeys when I remembered I'd left a pot on the stove. I rushed back to turn the stove off. When I got back to where I'd left the turkeys, they had vanished.'

'Did the turkeys ever vanish before?' asked Brigid.

'Of course not,' said the woman. 'Unless, of course, you are suggesting that somehow they knew they were going to end up as someone's Christmas dinner! Or maybe they just didn't fancy a walk!'

'W-well it is a long walk to t-the town, especially if - if you are a turkey,' said Sam. 'They could have guessed where you were taking them.'

'Of course they couldn't guess! I never even mentioned where they were going,' said the woman. 'Ordinarily they'd go by car but my husband is using the car for a sick cow.'

'It must be a very big car to be able to get a cow into it,' said Rory.

'Give me patience!' pleaded the woman. 'He wasn't putting the cow in the car! He was driving the car to go and look at her in the big field. He will be furious about the turkeys. Mrs Melia is one of our best customers. She'll be so disappointed. And I'll be at the loss of the money! The whole morning is wasted.'

Kate decided that this was the moment to try out the idea that had been forming in her mind. 'We have had a wasted morning too. We were hoping to make some money but we didn't. Maybe we can be of help to each other.'

The woman straightened up. 'Are you telling me that you'll help me find the turkeys if I pay you?'

'Not only that, but we will deliver them to the priest's house!'

'How much would you charge?'

'Four pounds,' said Kate. 'That's only one pound for each of us.'

'It's worth more than that to me,' the woman said, looking at the eager faces before her. 'I'll pay six pounds between the four of you.'

'Done!' said Kate, holding out her hand as she had seen the horse-dealers do at the local sales when they had agreed on a price. The woman slapped Kate's hand. 'Done!' she said.

A plan of action was quickly worked out. The woman would stay in the road in case the turkeys reappeared there. The children would fan out in different directions across the fields and call out if they saw the missing birds.

Kate, as she climbed the gate into the nearest field, thought, 'If the turkeys didn't get a fright and haven't got a secret hiding-place, why would they run away?'

Kate imagined the road as it would have been a short time ago. The turkey-woman was walking the turkeys. Suddenly she hurried back to the farmhouse to take the pot off the stove. The turkeys were left all alone on an unfamiliar road. They felt nervous. What would any sensible creature do in a situation like that? Head for home, of course. Home to the turkeys would be the farmyard.

The turkeys hadn't run away from the woman! They had run after her, only she had been too busy to notice!

Kate walked quickly down the road to the yard. A collie dog on a chain barked when he saw her. 'Good dog,' Kate said, not sure if he was being friendly.

There was no other sign of life in the yard. Then Kate heard a gobbling sound coming from a shed. She looked inside. Two turkeys glared at her. For an instant, she thought of calling the turkey-woman. Then she remembered a picture that she had seen of a woman leading two geese along with pieces of cord around their necks. If it

worked with geese, why not with turkeys?

She ran across the yard and into the house. On a shelf of the dresser, she found a ball of twine and a pair of scissors. She cut two lengths of twine and ran back to the turkeys.

'Don't be afraid now,' she said in what she hoped was a soothing voice. The turkeys huddled close together. Kate tied loose loops at the end of the pieces of twine.

'Gobble-gobble-gobble,' warned the turkeys but Kate refused to be frightened. Instead, with a speed and an accuracy that amazed her, she slipped the loops over the necks of the turkeys, who fluttered their wings in alarm. Then they calmed down and, as if carefully trained, they marched out of the shed with Kate holding the ends of the pieces of twine.

The collie's mouth fell open in amazement and he sat down with a thud!

As soon as she was out of the yard, Kate called out, 'I've found them!'

The turkey-woman was the first to come running down the road. 'Well, well,' she said, delighted. 'You're a very clever girl! Where were they?'

'In a shed in the yard,' Kate said.

'You can't be serious!' The woman looked as though she might imitate the collie and sit down in amazement.

'I took some twine off the dresser. I hope that's all right.'

'Grand! Grand!' the woman said. 'You'd best go straight to the priest's house now. Call back later for your money. If you were to wait while I fetch it from the house, the eagerness might go off the turkeys.' And she was right about the turkeys being eager! They were very anxious to start down the road, along which Brigid and Rory and Sam were now running towards them.

'They look like greyhounds waiting for a race to start,' panted Rory. 'Maybe we should shout "Go"!'

Sam laughed and yelled, 'Go!'

The turkeys reacted to the word as though they had been taking part in races since they'd been hatched. They moved quickly from a turkey trot into a turkey gallop. Kate could do nothing except run along behind them. She was afraid that if she tried to slow them down by pulling on the twine, she might choke them.

Brigid, Rory and Sam found it hard to keep up. They were already exhausted from looking for the turkeys. Now, to have to gallop after them and Kate, while carrying the mop and the buckets, was almost too much!

As Kate and the turkeys reached the canal bridge, Madge Cronin came cycling across it on her hill-bike.

For a moment, it was as if time stood still. Kate stared at Madge. Madge stared at the galloping turkeys. Then everything seemed to get speeded up as Madge screamed and swerved to avoid running into the birds.

This sudden change of direction sent her heading straight for Brigid and the boys. They scattered, jumping on to the canal towpath. Madge swerved again to avoid running over the blue bucket that Rory had dropped, and went free-wheeling out of sight.

Kate looked back in horror but could not stop. The incident with the bike, far from putting the turkeys off, seemed to spur them on to greater efforts. Kate yelled, 'Someone will have to go and make sure Madge is all right!'

Brigid got quickly to her feet. 'I'll go!' To the boys she said, 'Collect the buckets and things. Tell Kate to wait outside the priest's house!'

Rory and Sam picked up the buckets, the cloths and the pieces of the long-handled mop and set off after Kate, who was facing a new danger – traffic!

Now that she was on the outskirts of the town of Tobar, the road was no longer empty. Cars and vans and even the occasional truck rattled along. There was no proper footpath and, even if there had been, Kate doubted that the turkeys would have used it. They preferred the middle of the road where they caused the greatest inconvenience and attracted most attention.

Kate decided that the best thing she could do was to act as though what she was doing was perfectly normal. She smiled at the occupants of each vehicle, hoping that they would say to each other, 'Oh, look, there's Kate Nolan taking two turkeys for a run! What a sensible thing to do!'

But what would happen when she got to the priest's house? How was she going to make the turkeys slow down, much less go in through the gates?

Brigid, meanwhile, had caught up with Madge, who, as soon as she recovered from her fright at the canal bridge, had come to a stop several metres along the road. Now that she was safe, she was also very angry. 'I could have been killed! I could have fallen into the canal and drowned!'

Brigid knew that there had been no chance of either of these things happening but she thought it wiser to say, 'We're very sorry. You just came over the bridge without any warning.'

'Oh, so it's my fault now, is it? Well, just you wait! You'll pay for this! And so will Kate Nolan!'

'That's not fair,' Brigid said. 'How could we know that we'd meet you like that?'

'Because you knew that I'd try to find you . . . Or, at least, what I mean is . . .' Madge tried desperately to think of a way to wriggle out of the fact that she had admitted to Brigid Kelly, of all people, that she had gone to the trouble of looking for her and her companions.

Brigid suddenly felt sorry for Madge but Madge gave her no time to say anything else. Instead, she pedalled off into the countryside. There was then nothing more Brigid could do except set off after Rory and Sam who, by now, were dodging through the traffic trying to catch up with Kate.

Kate looked back and saw them. 'Get into the side of the road,' she called out. 'Try and pass me!'

The boys moved over to the grass verge and found it much easier to run between it and the cars. There was also less chance of tripping over the mop handle. When they drew level with Kate, she said, 'Make sure that the gates into the priest's house are open. Then you will have to think of a way to make the turkeys change direction and go in through them!'

The boys looked alarmed at these instructions. Then Sam said, 'The-the mop handle! We can bang the-the buckets on it. It'll be like a frontier barrier if we stand in the middle of the road!'

'We might get run over,' said Rory.

'No, we won't! The traffic is slowing down. There must be a traffic jam in the town with all the Christmas shoppers!'

Sam was right. Traffic was coming to a halt, making things more difficult for Kate. Now, instead of being able to run between vehicles, she and the turkeys had to go around them.

The turkeys, as they approached a large van, suddenly decided to run around different sides of it. Kate had the choice of pulling on the twine and choking the birds – or of letting go of the twine to avoid being bounced off the back of the van!

She let go of the twine!

The turkeys galloped on, unaware that Kate was no longer in control of them. Rory and Sam were in position in the middle of the road. The turkeys gobbled frantically as the boys bounced the buckets on the mop handle. They changed direction.

So did the boys, staying in front of the birds.

The turkeys swerved again. This time, they were facing the open gates of the priest's residence. The spacious garden and the tidy gravelled path looked so safe and peaceful that the birds exchanged turkey-eyed looks, gobbled in agreement and headed in through the gates, following the path around to the back of the house.

With shouts of triumph, Kate and the boys rushed in after them and slammed the gates shut.

7

Rory Meets a New Friend

The turkeys came to a complete halt and allowed Kate to take the twine from around their necks.

She and the boys were overcome by a great feeling of relief. This feeling became ever greater when Brigid turned up and reported that Madge was unhurt but very, very cross.

Mrs Melia, the priest's housekeeper, came hurrying out of the house. 'Well I declare, if it isn't the turkeys from the Anderson farm!' She clapped her hands in delight. 'And right to the second of the promised time of twelve o'clock. Just listen!'

The turkeys seemed to regard this as an instruction to them as well for they stretched their necks as far as they would go and listened as the church bells rang out the Angelus over Tobar.

'How do you kill the turkeys,' Sam asked.

'In as nice a way as possible,' replied Mrs Melia. 'But this year, I'm just wondering if I'm not getting too old for the job.'

'Of course you aren't,' Brigid said quickly, in case Kate offered to kill the turkeys.

'Ah yes, but plucking them takes so long,' sighed Mrs Melia.

The children were suddenly interested. 'We are in the service industries,' Kate said. 'We undertake jobs of a certain nature such as plucking dead turkeys.'

'Well, you'd hardly be foolish enough to pluck a live one,' Mrs Melia said and laughed loudly at her own joke.

'No, of course not!' Kate managed to smile. 'The rate

would be two pounds . . .' She paused to see how Mrs Melia would feel about such a price. When she did not seem worried, Kate said, 'That's two pounds for each bird. Four pounds for the pair.'

'Well now, that seems very fair to me, very fair indeed,' Mrs Melia said in such a pleased voice that Kate regretted not having asked for more.

'We clean windows as well,' Rory said.

'Oh I had those done yesterday,' replied Mrs Melia. 'But there is one small job you could undertake and that is to clean the priest's car. He has important calls to make this afternoon. Usually he would take it to the garage but it seems that the automatic wash there is broken.'

The four children's hearts jumped joyfully. The work opportunity that they had been hoping and praying for was suddenly being presented to them – car-washing! They had all the equipment that they need. The broken mop, instead of being of little use, would now be of great use for wiping windscreens.

'We will do the car now before lunch,' Rory said.

'As soon as we've agreed on a price,' Kate said quickly.

'I believe it costs three pounds fifty to have it washed at the garage,' said Mrs Melia.

'Three pounds fifty it is so,' said Kate. For a second, she almost held her hand out to seal the bargain as she had with Mrs Anderson, the turkey-woman. Then she decided that perhaps this was not the correct thing to do with the priest's housekeeper so she just smiled.

The priest's car was a fine big black one and the children set to cleaning it with great enthusiasm. The result was that, when they had finished, it sparkled and shone as though it had only just left the salesroom.

Mrs Melia was thrilled. 'I would recommend you to anyone that I know,' she said. 'If you do half as good a job plucking the turkeys, then I will be more pleased than I can say. Would four o'clock suit you to come back to start the plucking? I'll pay you all that I owe you then.'

'That's fine,' said Kate. 'Can we leave our buckets and things here until after lunch?'

'Yes, of course you can,' smiled Mrs Melia.

The children put the buckets and the cloths and the broken mop carefully in one corner of the yard. The turkeys, realising that Kate was leaving, ran over and stood in front of her like dogs waiting to be taken for a walk.

'No, no,' Kate said. 'You stay here!' Suddenly she felt quite fond of them. 'I'll see you later on.' Then she remembered that they wouldn't be able to see her. They'd be dead. 'Come on. We'll be late for lunch,' she said, wondering if the others felt sad for the turkeys. If they did, they said nothing as they counted the number of cars on the road that needed washing.

'Meet us back at the priest's yard at a quarter-past one,' Kate said to the Kellys when they reached the end of the main street.

When Kate and Rory arrived home, their mother said, 'Oh so you are back, are you? Where did you rush off to this morning? Your father had to drive out to Miss Freeman's with the note. She is expecting us to tea at half-past three. I want you ready to leave this house no later than three o'clock.'

Rory and Kate did a quick bit of calculation. If they met the Kellys at one-fifteen and left them at three o'clock, that gave them an hour and three-quarters for car cleaning. Brigid and Sam would have to start the turkey plucking without them.

'And don't forget you are helping to paint the scenery, in the community centre this evening,' said Mr Nolan.

'After the carol singing,' added Mrs Nolan. 'I just hope that you and Joe Deegan and Arthur Molloy will behave when we are on the back of Mr Rice's lorry.'

Rory's stomach lurched at the mention of his two friends. He'd promised to tell them everything that evening. He'd promised that they would all make pots of money.

'Mashed potatoes?' his mother said quite loudly.

'What?' Rory looked at her in surprise.

Mrs Nolan stared at Rory. 'Is there something going on that your father and I should know about? For example, where were you all morning? And is that mud or something on your sleeve? I've only just noticed it.'

'It'll brush off,' Kate said.

'I know it'll brush off, but what I don't know is where it came from,' said Mrs Nolan.

Fortunately, the door bell rang at that moment. Or at least it seemed 'fortunate' until Kate opened the door and found Madge Cronin on the doorstep. She stared coldly at Kate. 'I've a message for your mother,' she said. Then, without waiting to be invited, she walked down the hall and into the kitchen.

'Hello, Madge,' Mrs Nolan said.

'I've a message for you from my mother,' Madge said primly. 'She just wants to let you know that, for the moment, she would sooner I didn't go around with Kate. I was almost involved in a serious accident today because of Kate and Rory and the Kellys. But, even if I hadn't been in danger, she would sooner I didn't go around with Kate for the moment.'

Mr and Mrs Nolan received this announcement in silence. Then Mrs Nolan stood up and said, 'Thank you, Madge, for bringing us that message from your mother. Would you like anything to eat? Or have you had your lunch?'

Madge was clearly taken aback by the way that Mr and Mrs Nolan had received her news. 'I had my lunch at home but . . . what am I to tell Mum?'

'Exactly what I have just said to you,' said Mrs Nolan, 'Which is that I have thanked you for bringing us her message. Now, if there is nothing else, Kate will see you to the door.'

But Madge was not quite ready to leave. 'I saw them running across the fields with the Kellys. They were carrying buckets. They tried to knock me off my bike on the canal bridge.'

'We did not,' Rory said. 'It was all your fault.'

'Please, Rory, you know how much I dislike arguments at the table,' Mrs Nolan had never sounded so stern. 'Kate?' She indicated to Kate to open the front door.

Madge looked as though she might make one final attempt to cause trouble. Then seeing that Mrs Nolan was determined to have no further talk, she walked out of the house without another word.

'You were great,' William said admiringly.

'Was I?' said Mrs Nolan. 'I'm not sure how great it was to let that child annoy me.'

'You didn't sound at all annoyed,' said Mr Nolan.

'Well, I felt annoyed enough to give Madge a good shaking.' Mrs Nolan began to dish up a trifle without waiting for the others to finish the stew. 'How dare she and Mrs Cronin try to tell Kate and Rory who they can make friends with. But that is not to say that I don't want to know exactly what Rory and Kate are up to with the Kellys.'

'It's a secret,' Kate said.

'A secret that involves buckets and knocking people off their bicycles?' Mrs Nolan raised her eyebrows.

'We really didn't do that,' Kate protested. 'Madge came over the bridge so quickly that we didn't see her until the last second. Brigid Kelly ran after her to make sure she was all right.'

'Where did the rest of you go to?'

'On along the road into Tobar,' Rory said. 'But we didn't try to do anything to Madge. She's just furious because Kate won't tell her what the secret is. And the only reason it's a secret at all is so that a certain someone won't be disappointed if it doesn't happen.'

'An explanation that is about as clear as muddy water,' declared Mrs Nolan.

'We will explain everything as soon as we can,' promised Kate.

'Very well,' nodded Mr Nolan. 'Just as long as whatever you are up to isn't dangerous.'

As soon as they had loaded the washing machine, Kate and Rory went to meet the Kellys. They half expected Madge to be hanging around outside, but she wasn't. 'She must have gone home,' said Kate.

'Let's not take any chances,' said Rory. 'Let's split up and go as confusing a way as we can back to the priest's yard.'

Kate took a route that involved walking through the front entrance of the main supermarket and out of the back door. She then went around by the library, up the hill, and ran quickly around the back of the courthouse. Only then did she go towards the priest's yard.

Meanwhile, Rory ran along the many side streets in the town, pausing frequently without warning to look over his shoulder or to suddenly dodge behind a parked vehicle or a lamp post. So unusual were his movements that he eventually attracted the attention of a large, battered mongrel who began to follow him. Rory tried to shoo him away but this seemed to make the dog even more interested, not to mention friendly. He came closer, wagging a long rope-like tail.

Rory picked up a short stick and waved it at the dog.

The dog's ears pricked up, thinking that this was the

start of a game. Rory flung the stick as far away as he could. The dog bounded after it. Rory broke into a run, cut from one street to another and might have got away if he hadn't bumped head first into Joe Deegan and Arthur Molloy.

All three were stunned by the collision. Then the mongrel rushed around the corner, flung himself at Rory and dropped the stick at his feet.

'Where did you get the dog?' Arthur asked, rubbing his forehead.

'He just keeps following me,' Rory said.

'Dogs don't just follow people. You must have done something,' Joe said.

'I threw the stick to try and get away from him.' Rory kicked the stick towards Joe. 'Will you keep him here while I get away again? All you have to do is pick up the stick and wave it until I am out of sight.'

'OK' agreed Joe. 'But don't forget that you promised to tell us everything later on.'

'And so I will,' said Rory.

Joe picked up the stick. The dog immediately danced around him. Joe threw the stick almost the length of the street. The dog ran after it. Rory ran in the opposite direction and arrived at the yard of the priest's house. Kate and Brigid and Sam were waiting, buckets, cloths and broken mop in their hands.

'What kept you?' Kate asked.

'Nothing,' Rory said. 'Where are the turkeys?'

A loud gobble came from the direction of the house.

'She hasn't killed them yet,' said Brigid. 'She'll do it later on.'

Kate didn't want to think about the turkeys being killed. 'Then we will come back later on. Now where will we start the car cleaning?'

'At the carpark by the river,' replied Brigid. 'There's an old horse-trough there that we can use for water. We borrowed some washing-up liquid from our place.'

'Won't it be missed?' asked Rory.

'No,' said Brigid. 'Mam is too happy to notice that it's gone. Dad has just got two days' work at the lumberyard.'

'That's terrific,' said Rory. And off they all marched towards the river.

8
At the River

They were delighted when they saw how crowded the car-park was. They could not have picked a better moment to start looking for jobs. People who had been shopping during the morning were driving away. Their places were being taken by new arrivals who were in good mood, smiling and laughing. The first four people that the children asked agreed to let them clean their cars. Kate made sure that they also agreed to a price of three pounds fifty per car, payable in advance.

The serious way in which she spoke made the car owners laugh even more. They handed over the money, telling her that she had better make sure that her 'team' did a good job.

The first four cars presented ended up as clean as the parish priest's. Several people admired the work and asked if the children would wash their cars as well. They'd pay when they came back. Kate looked anxiously at her watch. It was ten minutes to two. 'Can you and Sam manage on your own while we go to visit Miss Freeman with our parents?' she asked Brigid. 'We'll come back here as soon as we can. Then you and Sam could go and pluck the turkeys while we take over the car washing.'

Brigid nodded in agreement. 'What about the money that the turkey-woman owes us?' she asked.

'We'll have to collect that later on before the carol singing,' said Kate.

'All right,' said Brigid. 'Now which car do we do next?'

'That one,' said Rory.

Kate shook her head. 'It's the one next to it.'

'No, it's not,' insisted Rory. 'It's the blue Cortina.'

'No, it's the blue Fiat, then the Toyota over there. Then the black Honda,' argued Kate.

'We - we should have written them down,' said Sam. 'There's not much use cleaning the wrong car.'

'We won't be cleaning the wrong car,' insisted Kate. 'I know what I'm doing.'

None of the others was convinced.

Brigid said, 'I think we are going to have to clean all of them. Maybe the owners of the other cars will pay us when they see what a good job we've done.'

They set to work with increased determination – slopping, splashing, wiping, mopping. They didn't notice just how wet they themselves were becoming in the process or how much water they had spilled on the ground. It was almost as though they had ceased to think.

They might have gone on in that unthinking mood if Sam hadn't suddenly noticed how little water was left in the horse-trough. 'There's not enough there to fill another bucket,' he said.

The last of the cars was covered with suds.

'There must be a tap or a pump for filling the trough,' said Kate.

'I-I don't see one.' Sam walked around the trough to make sure.

'Then we will just have to fill the buckets from the river,' said Kate.

A low wall separated the riverbank from the carpark. A short steep path led down to the water's edge. The river was very full, flowing past swiftly towards the weir beyond the bridge.

'We will have to be very careful,' warned Brigid. 'Let me go first. I'm the tallest and should be able to reach the water with the bucket.'

She stepped carefully along the path and knelt down on

the bank. Rory handed her the blue bucket. Sam and Kate held on to her ankles as she leaned forward dipping the bucket into the river.

Water rushed into the bucket, filling it instantly. Brigid strained beneath the weight. Rory leaned forward to help her get a grip on the handle. At the same moment, a great smelly darkness descended on him. He was almost deafened by a great gurgling sound.

For one terrible moment, he thought he had fallen into the water and that the smell and the sound had something to do with drowning. The bucket slipped from his grasp. He heard Brigid scream and Sam yell.

Then suddenly his sight and normal hearing were back. There was a loud splash that sent a wave of water over him. Dazed, he lay there, hardly daring to open his eyes.

When he did open them, he found to his great relief that he was still on the riverbank beside Brigid. 'What happened?' he managed to say.

'It-it was the-the dog,' Sam replied, sounding almost as dazed as Rory.

'What dog?' demanded Rory.

'That dog there in the river,' said Kate, pointing to where the mongrel that had followed Rory earlier was in the water.

'He's crazy,' Rory said. 'I never saw him until an hour ago. He started following me. Joe and Arthur were supposed to stop him.'

'They didn't do much of a job then,' said Kate.

'I think he's trying to catch up with the bucket,' said Brigid. 'I got such a fright that I let go of the handle.'

'He-he won't drown, will he?' Sam asked anxiously.

'No, of course not,' Rory said quickly, but he was not as sure as he sounded. The bucket was just yards from the weir now and whirling around in very fast currents.

The dog's head vanished under the water.

'He's in trouble,' Kate declared. 'We have to get help.' Followed by Sam and Brigid, she scrambled up the path and back over the wall into the carpark. The only person there was John, son of Mrs Grey from the bungalows.

He swung round from examining his car and his mouth tightened angrily. 'You lot again! I might have known it! Not content with ruining my mother's windows, you have now ruined my car!'

He pointed a finger at the detergent-covered bonnet of his car. 'Ruined! The car is ruined!'

'Oh please help us! We think he's going to drown!' Kate caught John Grey by the arm and tried to drag him towards the river wall.

John Grey pulled free of her grasp. 'What are you going on about?'

'It's the dog that followed Rory!' Speaking her brother's name reminded Kate that Rory was not with them! Surely

he would never have tried to get the dog out of the river
all by himself!

'Rory!' She called his name as she ran back to the wall
and the river bank. Boy and dog were both gone!

'Oh Rory! Rory!' Kate wrung her hands. Her eyes filled
with tears.

John Grey, pale as egg-white, jumped over the wall. 'Are
you telling me that someone's been drowned?' He ran his
fingers through his hair, trying to decide what should be
done. 'The guards,' he decided. 'Go and fetch the guards!
And the fire-brigade!'

Shoppers returning to their cars, sensing that something
terrible had happened, rushed to the river wall. 'What is
it?' they demanded. 'What's happened?'

'A child has been swept away in the river,' John Grey
said. 'Will someone please go and fetch the guards – and
the fire-brigade!'

'What's that there then?' someone asked.

Emerging from a barrier of bushes on the bank was a
figure that was without doubt Rory. Beside him was the
mongrel who paused every few yards to shake water off
himself.

'Oh Rory, you're all right!' Kate, followed by Brigid and
Sam, rushed to meet him.

The people by the wall were furious. They turned on
John Grey. 'You should be ashamed of yourself, giving us
all such a fright.'

John Grey was outraged at being blamed for what had
happened. 'I don't even know these children!'

'Oh no,' said a man with a van. 'And I suppose it wasn't
your idea either that they should go around cleaning cars
for money! Well, you'll not get a penny piece from me!'

'Nor me,' said a woman, going to her car. 'I didn't even
ask them to clean my car.'

Hearing the engines start up, Rory broke into a run.

'They are leaving without paying us!'

'But you still haven't told us what happened to you,' Brigid said.

'I just called to the dog,' Rory said. 'I ran down along the bank, waved a stick at him and called. He swam straight over to the bank. If you hadn't panicked, everything would have been fine!'

'Instead of which Mrs Grey's son says we've ruined his car,' said Brigid. 'We must have cleaned it by mistake.'

'Maybe so but we didn't clean all the other cars by mistake. *They* owe us money!' Rory jumped back into the carpark. He called out to the man in the van, 'You owe us, three pounds fifty.'

'Let your father pay you!' the man snapped back.

John Grey began to make strange noises at the idea that anyone should think that he was the father of such a gang.

'How dare you,' he said. 'I never saw them until this morning when they tried to fool my mother and her friends into paying them for cleaning their windows, just as they have been trying to fool all of us into paying them for cleaning our cars!'

Brigid and Sam lined up next to Kate and Rory. They looked wet and untidy and dirty, but they also looked very determined and, in a way, almost noble as they faced the grown-up world. Sam, in spite of being the youngest, now seemed to be the bravest, as he said, 'We did not try to fool anyone into paying us for cleaning their cars. We asked them if we could wash them and they agreed.'

'That's true enough,' said the van-man. 'Or at least it was in my case.'

'Well, it wasn't in mine!' said John Grey.

'Our car was washed without our permission too,' a young woman with a baby said.

'That was a mistake,' said Kate. 'We couldn't remember which cars we had been asked to wash, so we decided to do more rather than not do enough. You don't have to pay us, if you don't want to.'

'Well, actually, it's very well cleaned,' the young mother said. 'I was going to go to the garage and use the wash there.'

'It's out of order,' Kate said. 'That's why we decided to offer our services.'

'Well, in that case, instead of being cross with you, we should be grateful. Three pounds fifty, you said?' The young mother took the money from her pocket and handed it to Kate. All the others, including the van-man, did the same.

'Thank you! Oh thank you,' the children kept saying. They had thirty pounds!

'And what about you?' the van-man said to John Grey.

'What about my car is more like it,' John Grey answered. 'Who is going to wash the suds off it?'

'We will,' said Brigid. 'We'll have to get water from the river.'

'You are not to go near that river again,' the van-man said. 'One close shave per day is enough. Use the trough.'

'But there's no water in the trough,' said Kate. 'And no way of filling it.'

'Of course there is,' said the van-man. He walked to the side of the trough, placed his foot underneath it and pressed a pedal that the children hadn't noticed. Water came gushing into the trough. 'When I was growing up, there were still more horses and carts than cars on the road. We always tied up our horse here when we came to Tobar. That's how I know how to fill the trough.'

Brigid quickly filled the remaining bucket and poured it over the bonnet of John Grey's car. The suds vanished. Sam and Rory began to polish off the smears left behind.

All the grown-ups, except John Grey, nodded approvingly. 'That's a great job,' some of them said.

The van-man said, 'You will, of course, pay them now?'

'I only pay for work that I've asked people to do,' came the reply.

'Well now, if that isn't the meanest thing that I ever heard,' said the young mother. 'And so close to Christmas too.'

'Kindly mind your own business,' John Grey said. 'Now please stand back! My mother is waiting to be collected from the library.' He started up his car and backed out of the carpark.

'It's time I was off,' said the van-man. 'It's nearly three o'clock.'

Kate and Rory looked at each other in alarm. They were due back home in just a few minutes to go and visit Miss Freeman. 'We have got to go too,' Kate said to Brigid and Sam.

'Don't worry. We'll be fine now that there's water in the trough,' said Brigid.

'We'll be back as soon as we can,' promised Rory.

'Let's try and get into the house as quietly as possible,' said Kate, 'and change our clothes without anyone asking awkward questions.'

'All right, but I don't think we need keep things secret much longer,' said Rory. 'We must have nearly all the money that we need right now.'

'If Brigid and Sam clean ten more cars, we are home and dried,' Kate said, doing a quick bit of mental arithmetic. 'We'll have almost paid for the mops and buckets and stuff as well – only we are not going to say a word about what we have been doing until we actually have that glass globe in our possession. It would be like counting our chickens before they are hatched. It could mean bad luck. And talking of bad luck, that dog is still following you.'

Rory looked around. There was the mongrel, as big and as battered-looking as ever, but with an expression of love and devotion in his eyes. 'Go away!' Rory said.

The dog wagged his tail.

'Clear off!' Rory said.

The dog gave a friendly bark and tried to lick Rory's hand.

'Wherever did you get that beauty from?' The children jumped as they heard William's voice. He was standing at the corner of Rowan Terrace talking to Honor.

Honor said to Rory, 'You're all wet. You look as though you've been swimming in your clothes. What did you do with the buckets?'

'One fell into the river,' Rory said.

'And, of course, you went in after it,' William grinned.

'No, he did not,' Kate said crossly. 'There could have been a serious accident.' Then she closed her mouth in case she had said too much.

'There might still be a serious accident when Mam sees the state that you two are in,' said William. 'She's in the front room sorting out the pantomime costumes so you won't be able to sneak in past her.'

Honor, seeing the effect William's words were having, said, 'Couldn't you let them in by the back door?'

William did not answer at once. Then he said, 'I don't know why I should since they won't tell us what's going on.'

'We will,' said Rory, 'just as soon as we can. That's a promise.'

'Oh, all right then,' William said. 'Honor can distract Mam while I open the back door. You two dodge around by the lane, only be as quiet as you can.'

9

Visiting Miss Freeman

Mrs Nolan glanced at her watch and said to Honor, 'Rory and Kate are late.' She had had a good day. Most of the pantomime cast had collected their costumes.

'I thought I heard them come in the back way a few minutes ago,' said Honor.

'Did you?' Mrs Nolan folded the fairy queen's cloak and went out into the hall. Kate and Rory were on their way downstairs, looking as neat and tidy as if attending the start of a new school term. 'Well, well, wonders will never cease!'

'We thought you'd like us to look nice for Miss Freeman,' said Kate.

'And you were absolutely right,' said Mrs Nolan. There was a bleep from a car horn outside. 'That's your dad come to collect us. Where's William?'

'Right here,' said William, sticking his head out of the kitchen.

'Good. Then we may as well set off. We don't want to be late.' Mrs Nolan opened the front door and stared at the animal sprawled across the front garden. 'What is that?'

'That is a dog,' said William, struggling into his best tweed jacket.

'I know it's a dog but what on earth is it doing here?' Her question was answered as the dog flung himself at Rory with a yelp of joy. 'Get off!' Rory yelled. 'You'll ruin my clothes!'

He ran to the car and managed to get into the back and close the door before the dog could join him. Honor and Kate and William joined him in the back, and Mrs Nolan sat in beside her husband, who said, 'Don't tell me we now have a dog in the family!'

'No, we do not have a dog in the family.' Mrs Nolan's voice was firm. 'Is that understood, Rory?'

'Yes, Mum.'

'Very well. Off we go!'

'The dog is running after the car,' reported Mr Nolan, looking in the side-view mirror.

'Then maybe you'd better drive just a little bit faster.' said Mrs Nolan.

The increase in speed soon left not only the dog but the town behind as well. The countryside looked very dark and lonely. The sky became greyer by the minute. The fields were empty. In the distance, where the river curved and almost met the canal, a mist was beginning to rise. Honor shivered and moved closer to William as they arrived at the high walls around the Freeman estate. William squeezed her arm reassuringly and got out to open the tall gates that guarded the long water-logged drive. The house, as the car got nearer to it, seemed even more mysterious.

'Such a change,' Mrs Nolan said as she looked at the wild, neglected garden and the paint peeling off windows and drainpipes.

'Dad and I will soon take care of that,' William said, trying to sound as though he was not impressed by the great silence of the place.

Mrs Nolan pressed the door bell. Chimes echoed inside the house. 'It still works,' she said in amazement.

'I fixed it yesterday,' said Mr Nolan. A faint light was switched on over their heads. 'A stronger bulb there might be a good idea.'

The front door was opened by one of the kindest-looking women that the children had ever seen. 'Maureen, how lovely to see you!' She kissed Mrs Nolan. 'Please

come in out of the cold.'

The hall was not much warmer than outside. Its walls were lined with large portraits in heavy frames. Display cabinets, containing stuffed birds and foxes and badgers, stood on tables. A wide staircase curved up into dark shadows where more portraits could be glimpsed. 'I'm afraid the place is much gloomier than the last time that you were here,' Miss Freeman said to Mrs Nolan. 'I am relying on Mr Nolan to restore it to its former glories.'

'I'm sure Dave will do his very best,' said Mrs Nolan. 'Now, let me introduce everyone. This is my eldest son, William, who will be helping his father with the work here.'

'Hello, William,' said Miss Freeman.

'And this is Honor Redmond. I hope you don't mind her coming with us. She is Doctor Redmond's daughter.'

'I'm delighted to meet you, Honor,' Miss Freeman said. 'Your parents and I are old friends.'

'And these are my two youngest children, Kate and Rory.' Mrs Nolan pushed Kate and Rory slightly forward.

'Hello, Kate, hello, Rory,' Miss Freeman said. Then she looked more carefully at them. 'But haven't we met already? No, I'm wrong. We haven't met but I saw you and your friends this morning taking part in the turkey race.'

'The turkey race?' Mrs Nolan fixed her eyes on Kate and Rory.

'Yes,' continued Miss Freeman. 'I was driving into Tobar today to do some shopping when I saw them.' Her smile faded. 'Oh dear, I've said quite the wrong thing, haven't I?'

'No, no, there's no need to worry,' said Mrs Nolan. 'It's just that there seem to be a few things going on around here that Dave and I don't know about. But we can talk about them later on at home.'

'Well, now that I seem to have put my foot in it, perhaps

you'd like to come inside and I'll put the kettle on to boil.'

The sitting-room used by Miss Freeman was brightly lit and warm. It was furnished with old leather armchairs and sofas that were very comfortable to sit on. Framed photographs stood on the mantelpiece and on top of the piano.

'Do you remember the piano?' Miss Freeman asked.

'Yes, I do,' said Mrs Nolan. 'You had a music teacher at one time.'

'Oh yes, poor Mr Eves!' Miss Freeman laughed at the memory. 'He'd come all the way from Dublin twice a week to give me lessons but even the simplest piece was beyond me. But you were always musical. Did you keep that up?'

The two women began to talk. The others listened. The Nolans already knew most of the stories that Mrs Nolan told. Miss Freeman's stories of her life since her parents had died were stories about travel to faraway places and, in particular, about a long stay in Egypt working on an archaeological site. It was there that she had met the man that she had agreed to marry.

'But it was not to be,' said Miss Freeman. 'He was killed in a plane crash in the desert.'

She took a photograph of a handsome, smiling man off the mantelpiece and showed it to them. 'If he had lived, we might have come back to this house, or, anyway, not let it just go to rack and ruin. For a long time, I couldn't bring myself to even consider setting foot in the place. Then I began to feel homesick for Tobar.'

'And will you stay here?' asked Mrs Nolan.

'I'll decide that when Mr Nolan has finished his work and there is light and warmth in every room. ... Now the kettle is boiling so I can make the tea.'

With tea, Miss Freeman served delicious sandwiches and biscuits and encouraged the young people to talk about their future plans. William admitted that he was trying to decide between being a professional footballer and a carpenter. Honor wanted to be a doctor like her father. Rory liked the idea of space travel. Kate wanted to be a television news-reader.

'None of you ever mentioned any of those ambitions before,' Mr Nolan said to his children.

'There are a lot of things that have not been mentioned in our hearing,' said Mrs Nolan, suddenly remembering the turkey race. 'Now it's time for us to be on our way.'

Miss Freeman said, 'Maybe you'd like to see the rest of the house before you go. I'm sure by now that it has a great reputation for being haunted.'

'Yes, it has,' said Kate, anxious to postpone any talk with her parents about what she and Rory had been doing. 'Not that any of us believe it.'

'Maybe not,' said Miss Freeman. 'All the same, at times I find the place very gloomy, which is why I've created this oasis for myself down here.'

They soon saw what Miss Freeman meant about an oasis – an oasis in a desert of dark, silent rooms filled with the smell of damp and made more mysterious by furniture shrouded in white covers. In one bedroom, a lion's head, mounted on the wall, looked so fierce that it was easy to imagine it roaring out a warning at visitors. In other rooms, curtains hung in rags. Everywhere there were portraits of strong, hard-faced people.

'Are all of these your ancestors?' William asked.

'Yes. As a family, we seem to have gone in for having our pictures painted. Some of them are by famous artists,' Miss Freeman said.

'You don't look like any of them,' said Rory.

'I assume that is a compliment.'

'Oh yes,' said Kate. 'But how did you manage to get your rooms downstairs so nice?'

'Hired help,' said Miss Freeman. 'Out-of-work men that

my solicitor recommended. They moved the furniture from other rooms for me.'

Rory and Kate both thought of Mr Kelly and how pleased he would have been to get work like that.

'Your husband has taken on quite a job as you can see,' Miss Freeman said as they came to the front door.

'Don't worry, we'll manage,' said Mr Nolan. 'I'll start as soon as the Christmas festivities are over.'

'That will suit me perfectly, Mr Nolan,' said Miss Freeman.

'Call me Dave,' said Mr Nolan.

'All right, Dave. Thank you for your help. Indeed, thank all of you for coming out to see me. I hope you'll come soon again whenever it suits you. The telephone will be installed soon. In the meantime, if you are passing, just call in.'

'And you must feel free to call on us whenever you want to,' said Mrs Nolan.

'I'm sure my parents would love to see you too,' said Honor.

'Be sure to give them my best wishes.' Miss Freeman kissed Honor and then Mrs Nolan. 'Good-bye, Maureen. It was lovely to see you again.'

'Good-bye . . .' Mrs Nolan paused and then said, 'You know, I've got so used to hearing you referred to as "Miss Freeman" that I feel I should call you that too!'

'What nonsense!' said Miss Freeman. 'We were always Adelaide and Maureen to each other. And we will continue to be. Now, safe home!'

Miss Freeman waved as her visitors drove away.

Mrs Nolan waved back and then looked at Kate and Rory. 'Now, I've one or two questions of my own that need answering. What is this about a turkey race? Kate?'

'There was no race,' said Kate. 'We were just taking the turkeys to Mrs Melia, the parish priest's housekeeper. Mrs

Anderson asked us to.'

'Mrs Anderson who has the farm out beyond the canal? I didn't know you knew her.'

'We met her this morning,' replied Kate.

'And how did you meet her?'

'Just out along the road.'

'And she asked you, just like that, to take the turkeys in to Mrs Melia?'

'Not exactly. You see, she'd lost them.'

'Lost the turkeys?' Mr Nolan joined in the conversation. 'How did she manage that?'

'They ran after her but she didn't see them,' explained Rory. 'Then Kate found them in a shed and put twine around their necks so that they wouldn't run away again.'

'What?' said Mr Nolan, taking his eyes off the road to study the expression on his youngest children's faces.

'Careful,' his wife said. 'The mist is getting really thick.'

'It's not the only thing around here that's getting thick,' said Mr Nolan, but, all the same, he kept his eyes on the road until they were back at Rowan Terrace. Mrs Nolan, who had remained silent for the rest of the journey in case she distracted her husband from his driving, now continued her questioning of Kate and Rory. 'Were the Kellys with you when you met Mrs. Anderson?'

'Yes,' said Kate. 'In fact we told them that we'd meet them when we got back from Miss Freeman.' She and Rory scrambled out of the car.

'Hold on there just a second,' said Mrs Nolan. She placed a restraining hand on Kate.

'Please, Mum,' Kate said. 'The Kellys will be waiting.'

'You still haven't answered my questions.'

'Yes, we did,' said Kate.

'But you haven't told me anything.'

'We'll tell you this evening, after the carol singing,' promised Kate.

'There's scenery to be painted as well,' Mr Nolan reminded them.

'Yes, Dad, we'll give you a hand with that. And so will the Kellys,' said Kate.

'Ah, Mrs Nolan,' a voice shrilled. Coming towards them was Mrs Hughes with her daughter Sylvia, who, as usual, managed to look pretty and sulky at the same time. 'We seem to have chosen just the right moment to call. We need to talk more about Sylvia's costume. It still isn't right.' She opened the garden gate. There was a growl from under the hedge. The mongrel crawled into view.

'He won't touch you,' Rory said.

At the sound of his favourite person's voice, the dog lunged past Mrs Hughes, who screamed, and attached himself to Rory. Mrs Nolan was furious. 'I told you that that dog is not welcome here.'

'He must have come back and waited after we drove off,' said Rory. 'It's not my fault.' Then, suddenly inspired, he added, 'But since you insist, I'll try and get rid of him. Come on, Dog!' The dog, delighted by the attention, ran after Rory.

Kate said, 'I'd better make sure that nothing goes wrong,' and set off after Rory and the dog.

Mrs Nolan said, 'Honestly, what is a person to do!' Then, realising that Mrs Hughes and Sylvia were listening, said, 'Let's go into the sitting room.'

The two children arrived back at the carpark to find it empty of cars and people. 'Brigid and Sam must be plucking the turkeys,' said Kate.

But there was no sign of them in the priest's yard and the house was in darkness. Kate and Rory hurried on to the entrance to the lanes, where Madge was standing.

Kate and Rory slowed down and tried to look casual but it was clear from Madge's face that they weren't fooling her. Kate decided that she had better speak.

'Hello, Madge. I'm sorry if I upset you this morning.'

Madge said, 'I'm not allowed to talk to you.'

'But you just did,' said Rory.

Kate said, 'Please, Rory, don't interfere.'

Madge said, 'You are the talk of the town, going around begging.'

'Begging!' Kate and Rory were stunned!

Madge gave a nasty laugh. 'Oh now, don't tell me you thought you could behave the way you and Kellys did without people noticing. I'm surprised that your parents let you carry on like that! But, then, maybe they haven't heard yet that the police chased the Kellys out of the carpark this afternoon!' Satisfied that she had really upset them, Madge walked away.

The police! Rory and Kate stared at each other in horror. Then the dog put his damp nose in Rory's hand, making him jump. 'Go away!' Rory said.

'Forget about the dog for the moment,' said Kate. 'We have to talk to the Kellys.' They ran as fast as they could to the Kellys' house.

Brigid opened the door. 'Oh good, you're back!'

Mrs Kelly called out, 'Who's that?'

'Kate and Rory. Sam and I are going out with them for a while.' The four children hurried away from the house. Once more a river mist was filling the lanes.

'Madge Cronin says the guards chased you away from the carpark,' said Rory.

'Someone reported us,' said Brigid. 'They said we were making a nuisance of ourselves.'

'And we don't need two guesses to decide who did that,' Kate said grimly. 'It was Mrs Grey's son, John!'

'He also told them that we were begging,' said Brigid. 'Fortunately, they didn't ask how much money we had on us. We had cleaned nine more cars by the time they arrived.' She gave the money to Kate. 'We had to leave the bucket and stuff behind us so that the police wouldn't see them. We went back for it when we thought it was safe. But it had got run over. It was all squashed flat.'

'What about plucking the turkeys?' asked Kate.

'We-we went straight to Mrs Melia af-after we left the carpark. She had the turkeys all ready for us. It took us ages to get the feathers off. And it was freezing cold i-in the shed that she made us use,' said Sam.

'She also said that we had to take the feathers away,' said Brigid. 'She gave us a sack to put them in and told us she would pay us when we brought back the empty sack. We didn't know where to leave the feathers, so we hid the sack behind the courthouse.'

'We can empty it on the dump out beyond the canal,' said Kate. 'While we are out that way, we can call on Mrs Anderson and collect the money that she owes us. Everything is under control. The glass globe will be ours tomorrow morning!'

Rory was about to remind Kate about not counting chickens before they were hatched but then decided that, in a manner of speaking, they were already out of their shells. 'While we are in the lanes, why don't we go and look at the glass globe again?'

'Oh yes,' said Brigid. 'Sam and I want to see it too but we waited until we were all here.' She drew back from something in the mist. 'What's that?'

'It's the dog that fell in the river,' said Rory. 'He keeps following me.'

'Does he have a name?'

'I'm going to call him "Dog", until I find out who owns him.'

When they reached Mrs Foley's shop, it was as though time had stood still since the previous evening, with the mist just as thick and the lanes just as quiet.

The same golden glow pierced the darkness. Even Dog

was impressed by the stillness of the moment, as the children moved forward and looked at the glass globe. Then, without warning, the shop window was plunged into darkness. Mrs Foley could be seen standing against the light coming from her living quarters. She lifted her hand in greeting and pulled the velvet curtain across.

'She's closing the shop early this evening,' said Brigid. 'Maybe her arthritis is worse.'

'Well at least she waved. That must mean that she likes us,' said Kate.

Dog and the children emerged from the lanes and collected the sack of feathers from behind the courthouse. Then they set off towards the dump and Mrs Anderson.

10
Unexpected Trouble

Neither the Kellys nor the Nolans had ever been along the canal road so late in the day before. It was quite different now with the mist swirling around their heads and the last of the town lights far behind. At first, Dog seemed to enjoy the walk. Then he stopped rushing around and instead stayed close to Rory, often almost tripping him up by stopping without warning, as if to listen to something that could not be seen.

'This is spookier than the lanes or the Freeman place,' Rory said.

Kate, who had enough real excitement for one day without imagining things, said, 'There is nothing to be afraid of just because we can't see the fields. You don't surely imagine that, once it gets dark, all kinds of wild animals and demons come out, do you?'

Dog keened. Everyone began to walk quickly.

The dump was ahead of them now. The main gates were locked but there was a gap in the wire that the children slipped through. Dog made no attempt to follow them.

'You'd think he'd want to go after the rats,' Rory said. 'There must be hundreds of them here looking for food!'

'You are deliberately trying to frighten us,' declared Kate.

'Indeed, I'm not,' protested Rory, but Kate was already hurrying back to the road.

Brigid and Sam were just as anxious to get away. Brigid even thought she felt something run across her shoes but managed not to scream. 'Just empty the sack anywhere,' she said to Rory who was now carrying it.

Rory turned the sack upside down at the edge of the dump and shook it. The feathers slid out. A cold wind touched his face. It was like ghostly fingers. He turned and ran, almost stumbling over the sack, back to the others.

'I'm glad that's over,' he said.

'So am I,' said Brigid. 'So is Dog.'

Dog did indeed seem happier as they left the dump behind. He skipped playfully from one side of the road to the other.

'It must have been the rats that were making him so nervous,' replied Rory. 'He maybe heard them squeaking and scrabbling around.'

'Rory Nolan, if you don't stop talking about rats, I'll have a heart attack,' Kate shouted. 'I hate, hate, hate rats.'

'I didn't know you'd ever seen one,' Rory said.

'I've never seen a snake in Tobar either but that doesn't mean that I like them,' replied Kate.

'The rats wouldn't come near us while Dog is with us,' said Rory.

'Some help he'd be,' scoffed Kate. 'He's afraid of his own shadow. And you and Sam had better stay here with him. There's a collie at the Andersons who might not like a strange dog around the place.'

The two girls set off down the road.

Brigid said, 'I want you to know that Sam and I think you and Rory are great the way you've been helping us. I just wish that we didn't keep getting you into trouble, especially with Madge Cronin. You and she were best friends before we saw the glass globe.'

'She's too bossy.'

'I think I might feel bossy too if my best friend had a secret she wouldn't share with me,' Brigid said. 'Could we not be friendlier to her? Promise to tell her everything tomorrow?'

'I suppose we could – if she'll listen to us.'

The collie barked loudly as soon as he saw the two girls. A light went on in the yard and Mrs Anderson came out.

'Ah, there you are,' she said. 'I have your money all ready for you. You had no problems, I trust?'

'No, Mrs Anderson,' said Kate. A giggle from Brigid brought back to Kate how she must have looked racing down the middle of the road with two turkeys on twine leads. She nudged Brigid to be quiet.

'And Mrs Melia was pleased with them?'

'Yes, very pleased,' Kate said.

Brigid's giggles became worse. Mrs Anderson looked at her, puzzled. 'Will you come in for a while? Himself is out tending to the sick cow again but should be back soon.'

'We won't come in,' said Kate. 'We are carol singing this evening and collecting money for famine victims.'

'Oh, I love carol singing,' said Mrs Anderson. 'Be sure to tell whoever is organising it to call here. Himself will gather the neighbours and you can be sure of a right good donation.'

The girls danced back down the road to the boys! Things were getting better and better! Not only were they sure of getting the glass globe in the morning but they were also responsible for an extra large donation for the famine victims in Africa.

'Mrs Melia might even be home by now,' said Kate. 'Rory and I will bring the sack back to her. Then we will be able to collect the last of the money. We'll see you at the church at half-past seven.'

Brigid and Sam laughed and nodded in reply. They were too happy to speak. It was as though they were dreaming the happiest of dreams and that the sound of their own voices might wake them up.

They ran back to their house in the lanes and, without realising it, were singing a carol as they rushed into the kitchen.

'You sound in great form,' their father said.

'We are,' said Brigid. 'Why don't you come carol singing with us? And don't say that you wouldn't be welcome or that you haven't been to practice. You know all the words and Mr Morris asked specially last night if you and Mum would think of singing in the choir.'

Mr Kelly looked at his wife. She smiled, looking contented and relaxed for the first time in months, now that her husband had found even a temporary job.

'Why don't you go?' she said. 'You'd get to meet people. I don't mind staying here with Anne.'

'All right then, I will go,' he said.

At the parish priest's house, Kate carefully folded the sack and put it on the back doorstep. The house itself was still dark but that didn't worry the Nolans.

'We might see Mrs Melia at the church,' said Kate. 'If not, it'll do in the morning. What about Dog?'

'It's not my fault if he follows me,' grinned Rory.

Dog barked in agreement and led the way back to Rowan Terrace where, without having to be told, he snuggled in under the hedge out of the wind.

As they took off their overcoats, Kate and Rory could hear their mother talking to Sylvia and Mrs Hughes in the sitting-room. She was saying, 'Of course, I understand that it is important that Sylvia looks her best in the pantomime. There is plenty of time to alter her costume before the dress rehearsal. Now, if you'll excuse me, I have to give the family their tea before the carol singing. We will see you there, of course.'

'I'm not sure that Sylvia and I will be at the carol singing,' said Mrs Hughes. 'She may have caught a slight chill last night in that draughty choir loft.'

'Oh dear,' said Mrs Nolan, hoping that she sounded sad instead of pleased at the idea of not having to listen to Mrs Hughes resuming her comments on Sylvia's costume between carols. 'In that case, perhaps she should stay home in the warmth.'

As soon as the Hugheses had left, Mrs Nolan went into the kitchen. 'Honestly, that woman! She's more trouble than the entire cast of the pantomime and she's not even in it!' She turned the heat up under a pot. 'I thought we'd have some nice home-made chicken broth. It'll keep us warm and it's very good for the vocal chords. Anyway, you can't possibly be hungry after the huge tea you had at Miss Freeman's.'

Rory was about to point out that that tea had been nearly three hours ago but then decided not to risk putting his mother in a worse mood than Mrs Hughes had already done.

It proved to be a wise decision. The chicken soup was delicious and there was plenty of it. The children, including William, had three helpings. Mr Nolan had two. Mrs Nolan had one-and-a-half and, by the time everyone was finished, she seemed to have quite forgotten how annoying Mrs Hughes had been.

'It's William's turn to clear the table,' Rory said and, before William could disagree, Kate and he were into their overcoats, out of the house and headed for the church.

Dog had slid out of his hiding-place and trotted alongside them as though he had known them since he had been a pup. When he saw the crowd of carol singers by the lorry, he slowed down and faded away into the shadows of the cypress trees that grew around the church.

'Brilliant,' Rory said. 'That dog is brilliant! He knows exactly when to make himself scarce. There's Mr Kelly!'

Mr Kelly, hearing his name, turned away from Mr Morris, the organist, with whom he was talking.

'Well,' he said. 'These are the two people responsible for myself and Brigid and Sam being here. Blame them if I ruin the evening!'

'Oh now I'm sure you will be a great addition to our group,' said Mr Morris. 'I'm just surprised that we haven't met before. Let me introduce you to the others.'

By the time Mr and Mrs Nolan and William and Honor arrived, Mr Kelly was chatting happily to the other singers. He was especially pleased to meet the Nolan parents. 'My children and yours seem to have suddenly become the best of friends,' he said.

Madge Cronin stood sulkily by herself on the edge of the crowd. Kate walked over to her, determined not to miss this chance of ending their quarrel.

'Can Brigid and I share you book again?'

'It's not my book,' snapped Madge. 'It belongs to the choir. Anyway, Brigid Kelly knows all the words, so you needn't come sucking up to me just to try and make me talk to her.'

Kate felt her temper flare. 'No one wants to suck up to you! And as for Brigid wanting you to talk to her, why would she want that? You are the most selfish person I've ever met!'

Madge lost her cool as well. 'Oh really? And what about you? Since when have you been so goody-goody? You and your stupid secrets!'

Brigid said, 'Keeping things secret was my idea, mine and Sam's. I know you don't like me because I live down the lanes.'

Madge began to wriggle with embarrassment. She had been caught off guard and knew that other people were listening to what was being said. She lowered her voice, 'I don't care where you live. But Kate and I were best friends until you came along.'

'It all just happened so quickly,' said Kate. 'No one intended to upset you. But we will be able to tell you everything tomorrow.'

Madge hesitated. Then she decided to accept Kate and

Brigid's explanation. 'All right,' she said.

'We're friends then?' Brigid asked.

'Yes.'

Suddenly Kate remembered Madge's mother. 'What'll she say if she sees you talking to us?'

Madge looked even more embarrassed than before. 'Well, she didn't exactly say that I wasn't to talk to you. She'll understand when I tell her that everything is all right again.'

Rory was having to cope with a similar situation with Joe and Arthur, who, having waited for him in the toolshed at Joe's house, arrived at the church just as the carol singers were getting into the lorry.

'Where were you?' Joe asked. 'We waited nearly an hour.'

'I forgot,' said Rory.

'You forgot about a special meeting of the Demolishers?' Arthur said in disbelief. 'I suppose you forgot too that you were going to tell us how to become millionaires.'

Mr Morris saved Rory from having to answer as he looked into the lorry and said, 'Are we all here? Good!'

Kate leaned forward and said, 'The Andersons out near the canal said they would get the neighbours together to hear us. They'll give us a big donation.'

'Well then, we will certainly go there but, first, we'll tour the town,' said Mr Morris. 'Would someone please bang on the cab to tell the driver to move off?'

Mrs Nolan, being nearest to the cab, banged on it. As the lorry drove away, she looked very thoughtfully at Kate and Rory and said to Mr Nolan, 'Did you notice how seriously the children were talking to each other? And where did Kate meet Mrs Anderson again? There is something going on and I intend to find out what before this evening is over!'

The lorry's first stop was by the Christmas tree in the

market square. Mr Morris sounded a note and gave the signal for the singing to begin. People of all ages came out of the houses and shops and pubs and gathered around the lorry. They were mentally transported by the sound of the carols to other places and other times, and began to think what Christmas was truly about. They also thought of the hungry people in Africa and put as much money as they could spare into the collection buckets.

From there the lorry drove to the top of the main street, then to the busier of the sidestreets and to the shopping centre. Everywhere, crowds gathered to listen. Everywhere, people helped to fill the buckets. Mr Morris was very pleased, not only with the money but with the excellence of the singing. He once more praised Sam and Brigid and added, 'But, of course, now that I have heard their father sing, I know where they get their talent. Now it has

been suggested to me by Kate Nolan that we go out on a brief tour of the countryside. Are you all agreeable to that?'

There was no objection so the lorry headed out towards the canal and the Anderson farm. As they drove past the dump, the Nolan and the Kelly children looked eagerly over the wire to see if the headlights would reveal any rats but the darkness was pierced so briefly that they couldn't see the piles of rubbish, never mind rats.

In the Anderson farmyard, six cars were parked. At the sound of the lorry arriving, a large group of people came out of the house. The collie did his best to drown out the singing by howling at the top of his voice but then, as the singing showed no sign of ending, he retreated into his kennel.

The singers were about to begin the fourth carol when a

ripple of wind crossed the yard. Mrs Anderson, who was not wearing a coat, shivered. Then her face changed to an expression of delight.

'Look,' she said. 'Look! It's snowing!'

Singers and listeners gazed at the dozens of soft flakes hovering above the yard lights. 'It's like a Christmas card,' said Kate, lifting her face so that a flake might land on it. But there was something odd about the flake. It wasn't cold and wet the way a snowflake should be. Instead, it was warm and soft and showed no sign of melting.

Madge touched a flake that had landed on her coat. 'Feathers,' she said.

'What?' said Mrs. Nolan.

The money collectors in the yard fished the flakes out of their buckets and looked at them.

'They are feathers all right,' one of them said.

'How can it be snowing feathers?' a big, dark-haired man next to Mrs Anderson demanded. The children realised that this must be "Himself", home at last from tending to the sick cow. 'Is this someone's idea of a joke?'

'How could it be a joke?' demanded his wife. 'Aren't they coming down out of the sky? If anything, it's a kind of miracle.'

Then the pleased look passed from Mrs Anderson's face as she examined one of the feathers more closely. 'These are turkey feathers. You don't suppose it's a way of telling me that I ought to stop selling turkeys, do you?'

'Do you mean a sign from all the dead turkeys of the past?' asked Joe. 'I saw a video like that once, only it was buffaloes that came floating down out of the sky as a warning to the hero not to kill any more.'

'And I suppose before long it'll be cows that'll be landing in the yard to tell me not to take any more cattle to market?' said Mr Anderson.

'Maybe we'd best move on,' Mr Morris said nervously.

'I'm sure an explanation will occur to us all when we are feeling more calm.'

'Maybe there are those among us who could offer an explanation right now,' Mrs Nolan said grimly and fixed her sternest gaze on her two youngest children.

Kate and Rory pretended not to notice her but both they and the Kelly children knew that the most likely explanation was that the wind had carried the turkey feathers across from the dump.

As the lorry backed out of the yard, the collie dog jumped out of his kennel to bark. Then he sniffed at the feathers and jumped back as one of them landed on his paw.

Feathers continued to fall as the lorry drove on down the road. They caught in people's clothes and stuck to the side of the lorry. Then, as suddenly as they had started, they stopped.

'It is a most unusual occurrence,' said Mr Morris, gathering several feathers and putting them in his pocket. 'I have a nephew who works for the TV news. He's always on the look-out for unusual stories. I'm sure he'll be very interested in a sudden fall of feathers!' He peered up at the stars that were suddenly visible. 'I wonder if it could be, as Mrs Anderson suggested, a message but a rather different one to the one she suggested.'

'How do you mean?' asked Miss Green fearfully.

'Well UFOs, space craft,' replied Mr Morris.

'But why would a space craft use feathers to send us messages?'

'So close to Christmas. They might think feathers have a special meaning this time of year. I'll phone my nephew when we get back to Tobar. But now, since we are out this way, we might as well visit the bungalows and give the residents there a treat.'

The lorry stopped half way down Quarry Road. At the

first burst of singing, front doors opened and elderly people, wrapped up against the cold, came out on to the paths. Among them there was the deaf man who had threatened the children with the police. There was also the couple whose dog had made such a row when Rory had rung the doorbell. Then there was Mrs White and, next to her, Mrs Brown. Then there were the people that the children had never met. Then on the opposite side of the road were more residents, in the middle of whom stood Mrs Grey.

'Keep your heads down,' hissed Kate. 'That way we won't be recognised.' The others had no sooner followed her instructions than Mr Morris said, 'What is the matter with you four? You might as well be singing inside a cupboard if you don't stand up straight!'

'Kate! Rory!' said Mr Nolan. 'Do as you're told.'

'Brigid! Sam!' said Mr Kelly. 'Behave yourselves.'

Very reluctantly, the children raised their heads and found themselves staring down at John Grey, who had left the supper he had been eating in his mother's house to come and see who exactly had come collecting money for famine victims. His eyes glittered with a mixture of fury and triumph when he saw the frightened look on the children's faces.

'Well, well,' he said. 'What have we got here? Rogues and vagabonds out looking for money again!'

Mrs Nolan moved forward. 'I beg your pardon,' she said. 'Those are my children you are talking about.'

'And mine,' said Mr Kelly. 'Or at least I mean two of them are mine.'

'Well, that is not necessarily something to be proud of.' John Grey marched back to where his mother stood. 'Mother, let's go back indoors.'

Mrs Grey began to protest.

'No, please, Mother,' her son insisted. 'We are not going

to waste money on this lot!'

By now all the singing had stopped. The people in the lorry looked at the Nolans and the Kellys. Mrs Nolan had never felt so ashamed in her life but she managed to sound very dignified when she spoke. 'Dave and I are as much in the dark as you are – as I am sure Mr Kelly is – as to what is going on. But you can rest assured that we will do our best to put things right.' She looked at Miss Green, who, as postmistress, knew everyone in Tobar. 'That man, just now, what was his name?'

'John Grey,' replied Miss Green. 'His mother lives in that bungalow.'

'Has she a telephone?'

'Yes,' said Miss Green.

'Very well,' said Mrs. Nolan. 'I will phone them as soon as I get home. Mr Morris, is there anywhere else you want to go?'

Mr Morris shook his head.

'Then, if you don't mind, could we go straight back to Tobar?' asked Mrs Nolan.

11
Disaster!

You don't have to be a genius to guess what was the main topic of conversation in Tobar for the rest of the evening. As the carol singers climbed down from the lorry outside the church, they stared at Kate and Rory and Sam and Brigid, and then walked away, deep in conversation.

Mrs Nolan approached the children. 'I have had a quick word with your father and Mr Kelly. We think that it might be best if you went, as planned, to the community centre and painted some of the scenery. That way we will all have time to calm down a bit more.'

Mr Kelly said, 'Brigid and Sam will take their share of the blame for what's been going on.'

'But we-we didn't do anything wrong,' stammered Sam.

'That's right,' said Rory.

'Please, no arguments now,' said Mr Nolan. He and Mr Kelly led the way to the community centre. The children followed behind, with Honor and William bringing up the rear. 'We're like a group of prisoners being sent to Devil's Island,' said William. 'We even have a guard dog to make sure we don't try and escape.'

Rory looked back. Dog was at the end of the procession. He had waited patiently for the lorry to return and now had become part of the procession without attracting too much attention. Rory slipped back to him and patted his head.

'You really do believe in living dangerously,' said William. 'You might be shot at dawn if you are seen encouraging that mutt.'

'He is not a mutt,' said Rory. 'He is a very intelligent

dog. He even knows the name that I gave him.'

'Which is what?' asked Honor.

' "Dog",' said Rory.

'Dog?' William laughed. 'Well at least I suppose it's better than the man who called his pet zebra "Spot". Are you going to tell us what's being going on?'

'No,' said Rory. 'I am not!' He looked around to see where Dog could wait while they were in the centre, but Dog had already noticed a piece of old carpet waiting to be collected from the side of the building. He settled happily down on that and gave a slight bark of pleasure when Rory patted his head again.

The sound made Mr Nolan look back. 'What was that?'

'Sounded like a dog to me,' said William.

And that answer seemed to satisfy Mr Nolan for he asked no more questions.

Everyone threw himself into the work and, for the

moment, worries about what lay ahead in the house in Rowan Terrace faded. Mr Kelly proved to be brilliant at helping Mr Nolan to finish building some of the scenery and he had terrific ideas about patterns and colours.

'Your dad is great,' Rory said to Sam.

At ten-fifteen the centre closed, so the painting would have to be resumed next day.

Mr Nolan said to Kate and Rory, 'Tell your mother that Mr Kelly and I are going for a pint. I want to have a talk with him.' Then, seeing the worried look return to his children's eyes, he added, 'It has nothing to do with what you and the Kellys have been up to. Mr Kelly could be very useful to me when I start work out at the Freeman place.'

Mr Kelly said to Brigid and Sam, 'The two of you are to go straight home. Tell your Mum I won't be long. I don't intend to say anything to her about you being in trouble until tomorrow. She deserves one happy evening.'

'But we are not in trouble, not really,' said Brigid. 'We can explain everything in the morning.'

'And I'm to be included in those explanations, don't forget,' said Madge.

'We'll all meet in the market square by the Christmas tree at nine o'clock,' said Kate. She reckoned that she would have collected the money from Mrs Melia by then. Madge, and even Joe and Arthur, could come to Mrs Foley's shop and see the glass globe being bought.

Suddenly things didn't look too bad. If they could just make Mum understand! Maybe now that they were so close to buying the globe, it would be all right to explain why they had been doing what they had been doing. As soon as she was alone with Rory, Kate suggested this to him. He agreed that, if it became essential, they should tell all. Dog slipped in through the gate and snuggled down under the hedge as the children went into the house.

Mrs Nolan was waiting in the kitchen. 'Where's your dad?' was the first thing she asked.

'Gone to have a pint with Mr Kelly,' said Rory. 'I think he's going to offer him a job out at Miss Freeman's.'

'Well he can certainly use all the reliable help that he can get, although I would have liked him to be here while you tell me all about your efforts to earn money today.'

'If you want to wait until the morning, we don't mind,' said Rory.

'I daresay you'd mind even less if we never talked about it at all.' Mrs Nolan pointed at the chairs around the table. 'Sit! And no nonsense!' She took her place at the head of the table. 'I have had a very upsetting conversation with Mr John Grey.'

'He hates us,' said Kate.

'And why should he do that?' It was obvious from the way that their mother spoke that she knew all about the window cleaning and the car washing. She went over the details as she had heard them from John Grey. It suddenly became clear to Rory and Kate how what they had been doing must have seemed to many people. By the time they had got to the carpark, they must have looked like paupers' children just, as to John Grey, they had seemed like cheats and liars out to trick elderly people out of their money. And then there was Mr Rice at the garage.

'He is furious,' said Mrs Nolan. 'It seems that you told everyone that his car-wash wasn't working.'

'But it wasn't working,' said Kate. 'Mrs Melia told us.'

'It was out of order for about ten minutes,' said Mrs. Nolan. 'Yet, because of what you said, word got all around Tobar that there was no use in going to the garage. It also seems that people thought that Rory had been drowned! And what about the Kellys? Have they not got enough problems without the two of you leading Brigid and Sam astray?'

'But it is for their sake that we . . .' Rory glanced at Kate to see if the time was right to reveal the secret.

'For their sake? You did what you did for the sake of the Kellys? Kate?' Mrs Nolan waited.

Kate saw no way out of answering the question. 'It was really for Anne, their sick sister. We had an idea and we all agreed to keep it a secret.'

'It can hardly be called a secret now if the whole town knows about it. By the way, did you take money from Mrs Melia?'

'Not yet.'

'Mrs Anderson? Did you take money from her?'

Kate nodded.

'And the feathers? They had something to do with you four, didn't they?'

'I emptied the feathers from Mrs Melia's turkeys on the dump,' said Rory. 'The wind must have blown them to the farmyard.'

The memory of the Andersons standing in the yard as the feathers floated down over them almost made Mrs Nolan smile, but then she remembered how Mr Morris was going to telephone his nephew to put the story on TV. Everyone would be made a laughing stock unless he was told the truth. This could have a serious effect on the Nolan family.

'First thing tomorrow morning, I want you to give all the money back.'

'But we don't know the names of the people whose cars we cleaned,' said Kate.

'Then you can give the money to Mr Rice at the garage and tell him you're sorry for spreading false rumours.'

'It's Mrs Melia who should apologise, not us,' protested Kate. 'It was she who said the car-wash wasn't working.'

'How much money are you to take from her?'

'We didn't take any money from anyone,' said Rory. 'We

earned it just like Dad earns his money. And anyway, the money doesn't belong just to us. It belongs to Brigid and Sam as well.'

'I doubt if Mr and Mrs Kelly would want people to think that they sent their children out begging,' replied Mrs Nolan.

'No one could possibly think that,' said Kate. 'It's not fair to make us give the money back, especially since you don't know what we want it for!'

'Don't you dare talk to me like that!' said Mrs Nolan. 'You will do exactly as I have told you to do. You will give back that money. And now you will go to bed!'

Kate and Rory knew that when their mother spoke like this there was just no point in arguing. They also knew that to talk once they had gone upstairs would make things worse. They got into their beds, each feeling as lonely and isolated as if, instead of being in their rooms, they were far away from Rowan Terrace.

'I'll never sleep,' thought Rory.

In her room, Kate was thinking the same thing. She just wished that she was a small child again, so that she could have a tantrum and throw herself on the ground and pound and pound her heels on the floor. Then a great wave of tiredness swept down over her as all the events of the day crowded in on her. Within three minutes she was fast asleep.

And so was Rory.

12
Christmas Eve

It was going to be a very busy day in Tobar as people finished their Christmas shopping. But neither Rory nor Kate felt as though they were part of the excitement. They were deciding in what order to give back the money.

'We should go to Mrs Anderson first since we got our first real job from her – or at least you did,' said Rory.

Kate nodded. 'Brigid and I will go out to see her this morning. Madge might like to come along as well.'

'You'd better explain about the feathers,' said Rory. 'I hope Mum remembers to telephone Mr Morris before he calls his nephew at the TV station. What about Mr Rice at the garage?'

'I think we should all go there and explain what happened.' Kate divided the money, six pounds into one pocket for Mrs Anderson, the rest into another pocket for Mr Rice. Then they went downstairs to breakfast.

William and their parents were already at the table. They greeted each other but there was none of the usual chatter. Instead, what little talk there was sounded like headlines being read off a newspaper.

Mr Nolan said that, since he would not be starting work on the Freeman house until after Christmas, he would spend the morning in the centre working on the scenery.

A short time later, he said that he would be grateful if those who had been there last night would come along and help.

William said he would be along with Honor.

Kate and Rory said that they would be there after they had made some visits.

There was no need to explain what they meant by this. It was obvious that Mrs Nolan had told her husband and William about her instructions regarding the money.

It was clear too that Mr and Mrs Nolan and William felt sorry for Kate and Rory.

'But not sorry enough to let us keep the money,' thought Kate. That kind of thing often happened with adults. They insisted on certain things being done. Then they would see that, maybe, what they'd insisted on was not such a good idea. But somehow they weren't able to say so.

'I'll go and telephone Mr Morris,' said Mrs Nolan.

Kate and Rory took their outdoor things off the hallstand. Their mother had dialled Mr Morris's number and was waiting for an answer. Kate opened the front door. As she and Rory stepped out into the bright sunshine, Dog, forgetting the need to be cautious, emerged from under the hedge and flung himself towards Rory.

Before the front door could be closed, Mrs Nolan saw the animal. Any sympathy she had felt towards her two youngest children vanished. 'Hello, Mr Morris,' she said into the phone. 'This is Maureen Nolan. I need to explain about those feathers last night. Could you hold on just a second?'

She put down the receiver and followed Dog and the children to the front gate. 'I told you to get rid of that dog and what do I find? He's been in the front garden all night! Rory, you are to take that dog back to where you found him and leave him there! Do you understand me?'

Rory nodded miserably. This could well turn out to be the worst Christmas Eve anyone in Tobar had ever known!

Kate said, sympathetically, 'I'll tell Joe and Arthur and Sam to wait for you in the square.'

'OK.' Rory clicked his fingers. Dog, his tail wagging, followed him down Rowan Terrace, certain that there was some new excitement in the offing. Then he recognised the sidestreet where he had first met Rory. His tail trailed along the ground.

'I'm sorry,' Rory said. 'You have to stay here. Gosh, you must be very hungry! I'll try and bring you some food later on. Only you mustn't follow me.'

Rory ran out of the side street and into the market square. Dog made no attempt to follow him. He just sat where he had been left, once more let down by a human.

Joe had brought a football with him so the boys began to kick that around in a half-hearted way while Rory and Sam told them about the glass globe.

Close to the Anderson farm, Brigid and Kate were telling Madge the same story. Madge said, 'I wish I could give you the money you need but I haven't got it.'

'At least we didn't tell Anne about the glass globe,' said Brigid. 'Imagine how disappointed she would be now.'

'Every cloud has a silver lining,' Madge said in such a

serious way that, in spite of feeling so sad, Brigid and Kate had an attack of the giggles. 'Well I'm glad you haven't lost your sense of humour,' Madge said crossly.

The Anderson collie opened one eye and looked at the three girls as they passed. 'He's very quiet this morning,' said Kate.

'Maybe he's still in a state of shock after last night,' said Madge.

That made Brigid and Kate giggle even more. They were still giggling when Mrs Anderson opened the door to them. 'Well, well, if it's not the two of you back with a third, of course. You've just missed Himself. He's out tending to the cows. What about that shower of feathers last night? Did you ever see anything so wonderful!'

'That's one of the things we want to talk to you about,' said Kate. 'We were kind of to blame for that.'

Mrs Anderson listened carefully. When Kate had finished, she said, 'Well now, I won't say that I am not disappointed although Himself will be pleased that no one was playing any kind of a joke on us. It was very good of you to come out and explain.'

'We had another reason for coming out,' said Kate. 'We have to give you back the six pounds. Mum thinks you gave it to us because you thought we looked neglected.'

'Well indeed and I did not! I gave it to you because you saved me a great deal of time and trouble with those turkeys. I may have added a couple of pounds more because it's Christmas, but I can't take back money for a job well done. Maybe I could give it to you as a present?' suggested Mrs Anderson.

Kate shook her head. 'That'd just to be the same as taking it for the turkeys.'

'Well then, maybe I could give the money to this young lady,' Mrs Anderson nodded at Madge. 'Your mother couldn't object to that, could she? And she can't stop your friend lending you the money.'

Kate hesitated. It didn't seem quite right.

'It is the perfect solution,' insisted Mrs Anderson. 'So if I could just have the money back?' She held out her hand. Kate gave her the six pounds. She handed it to Madge. 'Happy Christmas, whatever your name is.'

'Thanks very much,' said Madge, 'and the very same to you.'

They ran back down the road, across the canal bridge and back to the market square at the corner of which they almost ran into Honor and William.

'We were wondering if we could help,' said Honor. 'William thinks your Mum was a bit hard on you. How much money do you need?'

'Fifty pounds,' said Kate.

'Fifty pounds!' William said. 'You really must tell us what's going on.'

'I can't,' said Kate.

'Why can't you?' Rory asked as he and the boys stopped fooling with the football and came to join in the conversation. 'Sam and I have told Joe and Arthur.'

'Because things might have taken a turn for the better,' Brigid said. 'Mrs Anderson gave the six pounds to Madge. Madge gave it to us. If everyone else does the same, we can still save the situation.'

'Only, of course, we can't ask people to give the money to Madge,' said Kate. 'And I don't think Madge should ask either.' She still felt uneasy about the way things were going. It was almost like cheating.

'What about Joe and Arthur,' said Rory. 'Could they ask?'

'We'd be glad to help,' said Joe in his best Demolisher voice. 'In a way, we might be saving someone's life!'

William and Honor became even more amazed. 'Someone's life? You're not talking about a ransom of some kind, are you?' asked William.

'No, but you could help us if you are willing to do so without making us tell you anything,' said Rory. 'You know Mr Rice's son, Matt?'

'Yes, but what has that to do with anything?' asked William. Then his puzzled expression vanished. 'Oh I get it. We are to go and have a chat with Matt who will have a chat with his dad, who, if we are very lucky, might give a present to someone that we know. Give us a head start of five minutes, then come to the garage.'

'Yahoo!' yelled Rory, knocking the football out of Joe's grasp.

The ball bounced high in the air. Arthur headed it to Joe who was almost knocked off his feet by Dog. The ball bounced again and landed at Kate's feet. Kate hesitated for a second. Then she kicked the ball as hard as she could. It soared over the heads of the boys to Brigid. Brigid passed it to Madge.

'Where's the goal!' Kate yelled.

'Here,' said Rory, taking up position at the entrance to a disused coalyard.

Madge was well ahead of Arthur and Joe and Sam.

Dog rushed out to meet her. 'That's not fair,' she screamed.

'Pass,' yelled Kate. 'Pass the ball to Brigid.'

Madge looked at Brigid. Then she did as Kate had ordered. Brigid dodged around Dog and kicked the ball straight at the gate. Rory caught it and kicked it to Arthur. Arthur touched the ball hard with the side of his foot. In what seemed like slow-motion, the ball went straight for the window of the courthouse. It bounced off the glass, which shook and rattled but did not break.

Joe caught the ball as soon as it landed on the ground. 'Enough,' he said. 'We shouldn't be playing football here at all.'

'We could have ended up paying for a new window with Mrs Anderson's money,' said Madge. 'It's time to go to the garage.'

Matt Rice was standing at the petrol pumps with Honor and William as the footballers arrived at the garage. 'You're out of luck for the moment,' he said. 'Dad had to go out on a job this morning. He won't be back until this afternoon. But I don't think you have anything to worry about. Honor and William have explained what has to be done. So just show up here at about three o'clock?'

'That's great,' said Brigid. 'We only need one more pound now. Mrs Melia owes us more than that.'

'I often see Mrs Melia in the shopping centre this time of day,' said Honor. 'I can accidentally on purpose meet her and have a chat! 'Go and wait at the priest's house.'

The yard of the priest's house was in shadow and quite cold but soon the sound of Mrs Melia returning was heard. She wasted no time in getting to the point. 'A young woman, whom I've just met in the shopping centre, tells me that, while I have been excused from paying a certain sum of money to certain young people, it is all right for me to give presents to certain other young people, so if those young people will hold out their hands . . .'

Joe and Arthur stepped forward. Mrs Melia handed them four pounds each. 'I know that is fifty pence more than we agreed but what's fifty pence between friends? A happy Christmas to you all!'

'And to you, Mrs Melia,' replied all the children.

As soon as they were back in the sunshine, Joe and Arthur handed over the money to Kate who tried to get rid of her doubts over the way things were going. None of the others seemed to be the slightest bit worried. Rory said, 'Only four-and-a-half hours until Mr Rice gets back. Why don't we go to the Community Centre and help with the scenery?'

Mr Nolan was already there hard at work. He gave each of the new arrivals jobs to do. Then William and Honor arrived and joined in. The place was filled with chat and laughter. The morning just sped by. It hardly seemed possible when lunch-time arrived. 'We should have this completely finished by this evening,' said Mr Nolan, 'that is if you all turn up this afternoon.'

'Oh we'll be here all right,' promised Kate.

'Good,' said Mr Nolan. 'Things seemed to have brightened up since this morning. You did do what your mother said, didn't you?'

'Oh yes, we did,' Rory said with a broad grin.

Kate remained silent as she and Rory hurried on ahead of the others. Rory at last noticed that she was worried. 'What's the matter?'

'I'm not sure that we are doing the right thing, taking the money as presents.'

'That's silly,' Rory said. 'We'll get the money from Mr Rice and go straight to Mrs Foley's shop, that is after I get some food for Dog.'

'Mum said you were to leave him where you found him.'

'Yes, but she didn't say that I couldn't go back there and feed him,' Rory said. 'It's our turn to clear the plates. If there's any food left over, don't throw it out.'

As it happened, there was a nice helping of mashed potatoes left in a saucepan, some gravy and scraps of beef. Mrs Nolan, who was expecting yet another visit from Mrs Hughes and Sylvia, excused herself from the table as soon as everyone had finished eating. She paused at the door into the hall and said, 'I'm glad you are not still upset at having to give the money back. It was the best thing to do.'

Her mother's kind words made Kate feel worse but she said nothing, just nodded.

As soon as William and Mr Nolan followed Mrs Nolan

out, Rory took a small plastic bowl from a pile next the deep freeze and emptied the left-over food into it. 'Dog can use it as a dish for water as well,' he said, and slipped out by the back door.

Dog was still sitting exactly where Rory had left him. He brightened up when he saw him. He became very pleased when the food was put down in front of him. He cleared the dish in ten seconds.

'You'll need water,' Rory said. An open gate led into what looked like a derelict stable. In the remains of one of the stalls was a pile of straw. A rusting tap was attached to one of the walls. He turned on the tap. It rattled and groaned and gave out choking noises. Then cool, clear water gushed from it. He filled the plastic bowl and placed it next to the straw. 'You'll be grand and snug here, much better off than sleeping under a hedge.'

Dog licked Rory's hand. His faith in humans was being restored. He decided to further test Rory's reliability by following him. 'I don't see how I can prevent you from walking around Tobar. I don't own the streets,' Rory said and rushed back to the community centre. Dog followed and settled down on the piece of carpet. It was a quarter to two by the clock in the hall. 'Only seventy-five more minutes,' Rory told himself, 'and the glass globe is ours!' He threw himself back into the work as did the others. Time passed even faster than it had before lunch. Madge put down her paint brush. 'It's three o'clock!'

'We have to go,' said Kate.

'Surely not all of you at the same time?' protested Mr Nolan.

'We'll be back,' promised Kate.

'And ready to tell us the whole story,' William reminded her.

'What whole story?' Mr Nolan was suddenly alert to the possibility of the children being involved in some new plan but, before he could question them, they had all gone, rushing out of the centre and along the crowded main street with Dog at their heels.

Mr Rice and Matt were in the office overlooking the forecourt. 'Hello,' Mr Rice said, 'so you are the unofficial car washers of Tobar!'

'We're terribly sorry,' said Rory. 'We thought your machine was broken. We hope you aren't too angry.'

'I was, for about five minutes,' Mr Rice said. 'It serves me right for not having the machine properly serviced. Now, I understand that there is a certain ceremony about to take place.'

Kate handed him the car-wash money. Madge, Arthur and Joe stepped forward. Mr Rice divided the money between them. 'Ceremony complete,' he said.

And so also, of course, was Operation Glass Globe! In spite of all the setbacks and worries, the children not only had the fifty pounds that they needed, they also had some money left over to cover the cost of the equipment.

Kate said, 'I think we should go straight to Mrs Foley's shop.' She hoped her doubts would vanish when she saw the glass globe again.

'Mrs Foley's shop in the lanes?' asked Mr Rice. 'She moved out this morning.'

'She can't have,' said Kate.

'All the same, she has,' said Mr Rice. 'And I helped her. That's the job I was doing. Her daughter was supposed to come and collect her this evening but, at the last moment, couldn't. She rang me to see if I could move Mrs Foley and her stuff to Dublin – and very strange some of the stuff was too. But at least she'll be with her family for Christmas Day.'

'The-the glass globe,' stammered Sam. 'Was there a-a glass globe in the stuff that Mrs Foley took with her?'

'A glass globe? No, she took no glass globe with her that

I could see,' said Mr Rice. 'But could you lot be "the Glass Globe Children"? If you are, she left a letter for you stuck to the door of her shop.'

Without pausing to even thank Mr Rice, the children got out of the office and ran as fast as they could to the lanes. The window of Mrs Foley's shop was completely empty. The letter that Mr Rice had spoken of was attached to the shop door. It was addressed to "the Glass Globe Children". Rory tore open the envelope and read the letter out loud: 'Dear Children of the Glass Globe, I have gone to my daughter in Dublin, earlier than I planned. I'm sorry about the glass globe. It was impossible for me to keep my promise to you. Sincerely, L. M. Foley, Mrs.'

'What does it mean?' asked Kate. 'Did she sell the globe to somebody else?' Then she noticed how upset Brigid was. She looked as though she might faint. 'Oh Brigid, we did our very best. I know it's a great disappointment that we didn't get the globe but at least we did our best. Just be thankful that we said nothing to Anne.'

'But that's just it,' said Brigid, in a small, quiet voice. 'I told her about it at lunch-time. We were so certain of getting it. And she looked so pleased . . . '

'Can we not get another glass globe?' asked Madge.

'Not like the one that was here,' said Rory. 'The one that was here was special!'

The children's mood was as dark as the clouds now creeping across the sky. Brigid and Sam were both on the verge of tears.

'We might as well go back and finish the scenery,' Joe said.

Like mourners at a funeral, the young people trailed back to the community centre. One look at their faces was enough to tell William that disaster had struck again. 'We were too late,' Rory said. 'The glass globe and Mrs Foley are both gone.'

'That sounds like a good reason to have a tea break,' said Mr Nolan. 'I want the truth, the whole truth, and nothing but the truth.'

When the full story had been told, Mr Nolan sighed and said, 'That is rotten luck, although I can't help feeling that letting people give your friends presents was kind of a cheat as regards getting the money back.'

Kate signed. 'I felt like that too. It was like deliberately letting someone believe something that was not true.'

'So we no right to the money at all,' said Rory. 'We can't even use it to buy something else for Anne.'

'Fifty pounds could make a great difference to the starving millions in the world,' said Honor. 'Why don't you give it to the famine fund? There will be a collection outside the church at midnight mass this evening.'

The rest of the afternoon dragged along. The excitement and laughter of the day had vanished. When at last it was time to go home, Kate asked if she and Rory could come and see Anne.

Anne, looking even more like a fairy princess waiting to be rescued, took the bad news with good humour. 'It can't be helped and it's a great idea to give the money to the famine fund.'

But, in spite of her cheerful words, the others noticed the sadness that lay behind them. 'She's only pretending not to be upset,' Kate said to Rory when they were on their way back to Rowan Terrace. 'She was really looking forward to getting the globe. Brigid must feel terrible. The disappointment might make Anne feel as though nothing good is ever going to happen to her again. It could have a terrible effect on her.'

13
Christmas Day

Because Midnight Mass was so popular in Tobar, it was necessary to get there early to be sure of a seat.

The Nolans arrived at half-past eleven to find the church almost full.

Kate paused in the porch and placed the fifty pounds in the collection box for the famine victims. The people around her were very impressed and full of praise but Kate was in no mood to explain where or how she had collected the money. Instead, all she could think, as she followed her parents down the main aisle, was that the adventure and excitement of the glass globe was all over. She smiled sadly across the way at Brigid and Sam, and managed a quick wave at Madge. Then the priest came on to the candle-bright altar and Mass began.

For a while, all the children forgot about the glass globe but, once Mass had finished and they were back in the cold night air, the thought of Anne came back to them. How lonely and disappointed she must feel in her room, hearing people call out greetings as they walked home past the darkened shops and pubs.

'I didn't see Miss Freeman at Mass,' William said.

'She's Church of Ireland,' Mrs Nolan said. 'She'd go to the Service at St Mark's. I do hate the thought of her spending Christmas Day in that house all by herself. I know I should have done something about it sooner but I was so busy with other things that I didn't.'

'Why don't you ask her to come and have dinner with us tomorrow – or, I should say, today – since we are one hour into Christmas Day?' asked Mr Nolan.

'None of you would mind?'

'Of course we wouldn't,' said William. 'She's very nice.'

'All right so,' said Mrs Nolan. 'I'll do it first thing in the morning.'

'I think Mrs Hughes and Sylvia are trying to attract your attention,' Mr. Nolan said.

'And I am not in the mood right now to hear another word from either of them about that costume,' said Mrs Nolan. 'I want all of us inside the house with the lights out before Mrs Hughes even manages to start her car!'

This command made the good-byes between the Kellys, the Nolans and their friends short and quick, with promises to meet later that day. Kate, seeing how down Brigid was, said, 'You mustn't be upset. What happened wasn't your fault.'

Brigid tried to look as though she believed this. Then she hurried off after her father. Mrs Nolan, who had heard what Kate had said, put a comforting arm around her. 'The business with the glass globe is over. Brooding over it will help no one, least of all Anne.'

Kate and Rory knew their mother was right but it was difficult to feel any happier.

Next morning, they woke to the smell of the special breakfast of waffles and bacon that their mother always cooked on Christmas morning. It was after ten o'clock, which showed how tired they were from the rushing around of the last two days.

'Dinner will be at three o'clock,' Mrs Nolan said as she sat down, 'so eat your fill now because no more food will be served in this house. That also means no sweets or crisps or anything which will spoil your appetite. I don't want all the hard work of getting dinner ready to go to waste.'

'We can all give you a hand,' said William, not really meaning it. He got a nasty shock when his mother said,

'I'm going to take you up on that offer. You can light the fires in the sitting-room and dining-room and keep them going. Then your Dad can help you put the extra leaf in the dining-room table. Then you can start to set it.'

William's mouth fell open in dismay. 'And what are Kate and Rory going to do?'

'They are going to take a written invitation out to Miss Freeman,' replied Mrs Nolan.

'By the time they get back from there, the morning will be over and I'll have done all the work!'

'It might not take them as long as you imagine,' Mr Nolan said mysteriously. 'But explanations can wait until after breakfast.'

William raised an eyebrow at Kate and Rory. They shook their heads to show that they didn't know what their father meant. Meanwhile, for the remainder of breakfast, Mr and Mrs Nolan kept giving each other what they hoped were secret smiles.

When at last the plates were emptied, leaving, Rory noticed, nothing for Dog, and the washing-up machine had been loaded, Mr Nolan said, 'Now you all know that the custom in this house is for presents to be opened in the sitting-room after dinner. Today, things are going to be a bit different for Kate and Rory. So, if they will just follow us – you are welcome to come too, William – all will be explained.'

Mr Nolan went out into the front garden and opened the garage which was usually too full with bits of lumber and tools to put the car in it. A large green dust-sheet was stretched over what could be a pile of planks. Mr Nolan swung the dust-sheet up into the air like a magician with a cape.

Instead of revealing a bunch of flowers or a dove, Mr Nolan pointed to a pair of new, shining bicycles. He and Mrs Nolan said, 'Happy Christmas'. Then it seemed as if everyone was hugging everyone else. 'They are wonderful,' Kate said, 'just wonderful!'

'And you had no idea what we were going to give you?' asked Mr Nolan.

'No, we didn't,' Rory said.

'We saw how much use Madge Cronin got from her bike. That was what made us decide. Now, while I write the note to Miss Freeman, why don't you take them on a trial run around the town?' said Mrs Nolan. 'There won't be much traffic at this time on a Christmas morning.'

There was, in fact, no traffic at all. Nor were any of the shops open. The only people on the streets were children and young people showing their presents to each other. The Nolans' new bicycles attracted a great deal of attention and admiration as they rode to the market square where their friends were waiting for them.

Brigid and Sam looked very smart in new sweaters that their mother had knitted. They had also been given two books by their favourite writers. 'And Anne got a book too,' said Brigid.

'So is everything all right?' asked Rory.

'K-kind of,' Sam said. 'Anne s-seems v-v-ery tired this morning. We might have to se-end for Doctor Redmond.'

Send for the doctor on Christmas Day! Anne must really be feeling awful!

'Do you want a go on my bike?' Rory asked quickly, in the hope that might lift the gloom that had suddenly come over them all.

'Y-yes I-I do,' Sam said.

Rory held the handlebars and Brigid gripped the saddle as Sam began to wobble around the square. Then Arthur and Joe had a go while Brigid and Madge tried Kate's bicycle. By the time they had finished, the glass globe and Anne seemed to have been forgotten again.

'We have to go on a message now,' Kate said to Brigid.

'Why don't you and Sam call around to our house this evening? Our Aunt Nora always sends us a new game at Christmas. We could play that.'

'We'll have to wait and see how things are at home,' Brigid said. 'But thanks for asking us.' The sadness came back to the group as Brigid spoke.

Kate and Rory cycled in silence to Rowan Terrace to collect the invitation for Miss Freeman. 'Be careful,' said their mother. 'The roads outside the town might be very slippery.'

But the roads to the Freeman place were very easy to cycle along. It was the avenue up to the house that was the problem. The pot-holes and mud that had been soft and squashy on the previous visit were now frozen hard. Cycling over them was very tricky.

'Another land, another age,' Rory said as he got off his bicycle at the house.

'What do you mean by that?' Kate asked.

'I'm not sure,' Rory replied. He often made remarks that were both serious and funny. 'Maybe travelling down the avenue is like coming into the past. Maybe we will find something out.' He rang the bell. Chimes echoed through the house. 'They sound like sleigh bells today.'

Miss Freeman opened the door and was delighted to see them. 'Come in, come in,' she said. 'I wasn't expecting any visitors today.'

'We have a message for you from Mum,' Kate said as they followed Miss Freeman into the living-room where there was no sign that it was Christmas.

Miss Freeman opened the envelope and read the note. 'Your mother has very kindly invited me to spend the rest of the day with you, and I accept with the greatest pleasure. It'll take me a short while to get organised but then we can drive back together.'

'We have our new bikes,' said Kate proudly. 'Look . . . so

we don't need a lift.'

As the children cycled back towards Tobar, Kate said, 'Well, did you find out anything new?'

'Not new exactly,' replied Rory, 'but just how nice it is to be nice to other people. Anne Kelly might be sick but at least she isn't all by herself, as Miss Freeman would have been if Mum hadn't invited her to our house.'

'You're right,' Kate said. 'And we probably saved dozens of lives by giving the famine fund the fifty pounds.'

Icy surfaces, pot-holes, ridges and slippery bits seemed to have vanished from the avenue. Kate and Rory would not have been surprised if Santa Claus had appeared over the tops of the trees with his sleigh. They were back home in less than fifteen minutes.

'She said she'd love to come,' said Kate.

'Good,' said Mrs Nolan.

Miss Freeman drove up shortly afterwards, wearing her prettiest frock and carrying a present in a box wrapped in tissue paper. 'I'm afraid that I had no proper wrapping paper,' she explained.

'Now you shouldn't have bothered at all,' said Mrs Nolan, putting the present under the tree with the others. 'You'll have a glass of sherry? Dinner won't be too long.'

Dinner, when it was served, was delicious and eaten with lots of laughter and stories and jokes. Some of the funniest were told by Miss Freeman, who turned out to have a great sense of humour.

'And now for one of the highlights of the afternoon, the unwrapping of the Christmas presents,' said Mr Nolan. 'Kate and Rory have had their main presents already but I think that there are still a few packages with their names on them.'

And Mr Nolan was right. There were several packages for Kate and Rory containing books and records and, as expected, a new game from their Aunt Nora, called 'Weirdo'.

'I hope Sam and Brigid remember to come around,' said Kate as she and Rory studied the rules of the game.

As if in response to a signal, the door bell rang. Rory ran to open it. Sam and Brigid were outside. 'We're not too early, are we?' asked Brigid.

'No, perfect timing,' said Rory, bringing them into the sitting-room where they were introduced to, and shyly shook hands with, Miss Freeman.

'Their father will be giving me a hand with the work out at your place,' said Mr Nolan.

'Good,' said Miss Freeman.

The children exchanged delighted glances.

'And now this is for you!' Mrs. Nolan handed Miss Freeman a bottle of perfume that she had found upstairs and wrapped while the children were delivering the invitation.

'And this is for all of you,' said Miss Freeman, handing the tissue-wrapped box to Mrs Nolan.

Mrs Nolan removed the tissue paper and opened the box. She stared at the contents for a moment. Then she looked at the children and said, 'It's the glass globe!'

Miss Freeman glanced around the room. 'You know about the glass globe?'

'Yes,' said Mrs Nolan as she very carefully lifted the globe out of its box and held it up to the lights. It was even more beautiful than the children remembered it as being. 'The children saw it in Mrs Foley's shop and told us all about it.'

'And that is where I got it from,' said Miss Freeman.

'I suppose you offered her more money than we did,' said Rory.

'I didn't offer her any money at all,' said Miss Freeman. 'I didn't need to. The glass globe belongs to me.'

'But how did it end up in Mrs Foley's?' asked William.

'Well, as you know, my house has been locked up for many years, visited only by my solicitor. When I moved back in recently, everything seemed to be as it should be with one exception. That was the glass globe that always hung in my father's study. I was allowed into the study only very rarely. The servants were never allowed in at all. Neither were any visitors, otherwise your mother would have known where the glass globe had come from.'

'That's true,' said Mrs Nolan. 'There certainly could not be another one like it in the world. No wonder the children wanted to buy it.'

'But they didn't want it for themselves,' said William. 'They wanted it for Anne Kelly.'

'Let Miss Freeman finish her story first,' said Mr Nolan. 'Then it can be the turn of the others.'

'There's not a great deal more to tell,' said Miss Freeman. 'Mrs Foley's brother worked for my parents as an

odd job man. It was he who put the covers on the furniture and saw that the house was locked up before he gave
the keys back to the solicitor. But, before he did that, I
think he helped himself to a souvenir. He probably never
thought of it as "stealing", but just "took" the glass globe
without realising how much history was attached to it.'

'Has the history something to do with the West Indies?'
asked Kate. 'That's what the scene inside the globe
reminded us of.'

'Yes,' said Miss Freeman. 'The globe has to do with the
West Indies. My family owned sugar plantations there. It's
been in the family ever since, or so I imagined until I went
in to Mrs Foley's yesterday to see how her brother was. I
thought I might offer him his old job back. When I saw the
glass globe in the window, I almost lost my temper but I
calmed down when I realised that she had no idea where
it had come from.'

'She told us that she found it in a box in the attic,' said
Rory.

'And so she did, in a box that her brother brought with
him when he came to live with her and which remained
unopened until after he died nearly eight years ago,
something of which I knew nothing until yesterday.'

'And she gave you the globe back?' This question came
from Mr Nolan.

'Yes,' said Miss Freeman.

'But should you now be giving it to us?' asked William
and then, realising that might sound rude, he said, 'I
mean, if it's been in your family for such a long time?'

'I'm not very proud that my family made its fortune
from the sugar plantations,' replied Miss Freeman. 'They
must have owned slaves. There was probably a great deal
of cruelty involved. I can't prove that. Neither can I
change the past, but when your mother invited me here
today, and I saw the box containing the glass globe on my

table, it seemed like a sign to me that I should use the globe to make someone happy. It seemed to be waiting there to be given away as a present.' She smiled at the four youngest children. 'And yet it seems as though it has not yet found its new home. Tell me about Anne Kelly.'

She listened carefully and sometimes laughed, as did the other listeners, while Sam and Brigid and Rory and Kate told how they tried to raise the money to buy the glass globe.

When the story was finished, Miss Freeman looked at Mr and Mrs Nolan. The latter said, 'I think the globe had better go to Anne. I hope you won't mind?'

'No,' said Miss Freeman. 'I won't mind in the least. It should be brought around to her immediately by the children.'

'They might drop it,' said William.

'Perhaps you would carry it,' said Mrs Nolan.

While the globe was being put back in its box and overcoats were being donned in the hall, Rory slipped out into the yard where he had left a big bag of scraps for Dog. 'If only I could find somewhere for him to live,' he thought. Then he had a wonderful idea! 'I wonder if Miss Freeman likes dogs!' He was certain that she would! He'd ask her when he got back!

The streets of Tobar were empty apart from William leading the four children towards the lanes. Mr Kelly opened the door. 'It's the glass globe for Anne,' said Brigid.

'W-we got it from Miss Freeman,' said Sam.

They climbed the narrow stairs, which, after the bright lights of Rowan Terrace, was even more like climbing up the inside of a dark tower.

Mrs Kelly was seated by Anne's bed. Anne's eyes were closed. Mrs Kelly straightened up angrily when she saw who the visitors were. She said, 'Anne is not to be disturbed.' For an instant, it seemed as though she might add, 'Have you not upset her enough as it is with your promises?'

Mr Kelly said in a voice that was both surprised and serious, 'They've brought the glass globe.'

Anne's eyes flickered open. She said in a faint voice, 'The glass globe?'

'Yes,' said Kate as William put the box on the bed and carefully took out the globe.

Anne stared at it, as enchanted as the children had been when they first saw it that misty night in the lanes.

'It will be even nicer when Dad hangs it from the ceiling,' Sam said. Then he grinned as he realised that, for the first time that day, his stammer was under control.

Mr Kelly rushed downstairs for a hammer and some hooks. Within minutes, the glass globe was swaying gently from the centre of the ceiling. Anne sat up in bed and suddenly looked brighter and stronger.

The glass globe, or maybe just knowing that so many people cared about her, was already making her feel better. She said, 'I don't know how to thank you all.'

'Now you mustn't overtire yourself,' said Mrs Kelly, as tears of happiness filled her eyes.

That seemed like the right time for the others to leave. 'Can Brigid and Sam come back to our house?' asked Kate. 'We haven't even tried the new game yet.'

'Yes, of course, they can,' said Mrs Kelly.

'Where's Rory?' asked William.

'He slipped away as soon as the glass globe was safely in place,' said Mr Kelly. 'He was carrying something in a paper bag.'

'He's gone to see Dog,' said Kate.

Great white shapes were falling over Tobar as William and the others walked along the lanes. 'It's snowing,' said Kate. Then she caught a flake and tasted it just to make sure that it wasn't a feather.

Rory did the very same in the stables while Dog wolfed down the scraps.

Then he looked up at the snow clouds that blocked out the moon and the stars. The stable yard was very dark. Rory thought, 'I don't feel nervous! I am in a dark shadowy place all by myself and I don't feel nervous!'

He gave Dog some fresh water. Then he said to him, 'I am not making any definite promises but I think I might be able to find you a home with a very nice lady! Now come on! You could use a bit of exercise!'

Rory and Dog ran through the streets, leaving a pattern of shoes and paws on the snow, that was covering not just Tobar but also the countryside and the road to St Patrick's Well, from which the town got its name. Tobar is the Irish word for 'well'. At the market square, they met the others.

'Now what are you up to?' asked William.

'Nothing,' said Rory. 'Just looking forward to tomorrow!'

And Dog barked in agreement.

TONY HICKEY is one of Ireland's leading authors for children. This is his tenth book for The Children's Press. The others are:

The Matchless Mice
The Matchless Mice's Adventure
The Matchless Mice in Space
The Matchless Mice's Space Project
The Black Dog
Flip 'n' Flop
More about Flip 'n'Flop
Adventures with Flip 'n' Flop
The Castle of Dreams

He is a founder-member of the Irish Children's Book Trust and a co-founder of The Children's Press.

TONY HICKEY

Flip 'n' Flop

In which the two little border terriers – Flip who
is 'for ever flipping around the place, trying to
find out what things are about' and Flop who is
'for ever flopping over and wanting to sleep' –
come all the way from Scotland to start a new
life with Frank in the Wicklow hills.

About their friends and enemies, and
their moment of high drama when the floods
come . . .

More about Flip 'n' Flop

In which the two terriers come to live above
Killiney Bay, sample the delights of swimming
and fishing, take exciting walks through new
unexplored territory, learn about old hunting
techniques and exchange experiences at that
best of all animal clubs – the vet's.

But can they come to terms with the cat next
door (Catriona) and Frank's father who just
doesn't seem to like them . . .?

TONY HICKEY

The Matchless Mice

The story of the Matchless Mice begins at Mangold Mansion, with Grandfather and Grandmother and Moaner and Flap and little Scratch and Old Crumbs who is always making trouble) and the two strange mice who come to call and Fred who turns out to be the most surprising character of all...

The Matchless Mice's Adventure

Mangold Mansion is under threat from an earth-eating monster, and the mice are under threat from the TCG (Tough Cat Gang). No wonder they sent an SOS, by magpie, to Arán: 'Come at once. We are in terrible danger...'

The Matchless Mice in Space

Enter Gladys, the beautiful mouse from Glitter, who is being pursued by the Creatures from Beyond the Sun. Naturally Scratch volunteers to help and he and Fred and Arán have an action-packed time as they fight off the Creatures *and* the treacherous Tough Cat duo, Nixer and Jamser...